Sugarplums

and

Second Chances

Jill Kemerer

Copyright © 2018 by Ripple Effect Press, LLC.

This novella was previously published in the *I'll Be Home For Christmas* novella collection.

All rights reserved. No part of this publication may be reproduced, distributed or transmitted in any form or by any means, including photocopying, recording, or other electronic or mechanical methods, without the prior written permission of the publisher, except in the case of brief quotations embodied in critical reviews and certain other noncommercial uses permitted by copyright law. For permission requests, write to the publisher, addressed "Attention: Permissions Coordinator."

Jill Kemerer
c/o Ripple Effect Press
P.O. Box 2802
Whitehouse, OH 43571

This is a work of fiction. Names, characters, businesses, places, events, locales, and incidents are either the products of the author's imagination or used in a fictitious manner. Any resemblance to actual persons, living or dead, or actual events is purely coincidental.

Scriptures taken from the Holy Bible, New International Version®, NIV®. Copyright © 1973, 1978, 1984, 2011 by Biblica, Inc.™ Used by permission of Zondervan. All rights reserved worldwide. www.zondervan.com The "NIV" and "New International Version" are trademarks registered in the United States Patent and Trademark Office by Biblica.

Cover Design by Ripple Effect Press, LLC
Interior Design by Ripple Effect Press, LLC
Cover Photo by Roberto Nickson (@g) on Unsplash
www.jillkemerer.com

Sugarplums and Second Chances/ Jill Kemerer. -- 1st ed.
ISBN 978-0-9978179-3-5

For my husband, Scott.

You make every Christmas sparkle.

The Lord is close to the brokenhearted and saves those who are crushed in spirit.

−PSALM 34:18 (NIV)

Contents

Chapter One 1
Chapter Two 9
Chapter Three 17
Chapter Four 25
Chapter Five 33
Chapter Six 41
Chapter Seven 49
Chapter Eight 57
Chapter Nine 65
Chapter Ten 73
Chapter Eleven 81
Chapter Twelve 87
Chapter Thirteen 95
Epilogue 103
Acknowledgments 106
Dear Reader 107
About the Author 108
More Books by Jill Kemerer 109

Chapter One

Chase McGill had officially become the odd man out. All the lost time he'd planned to make up for was disappearing as quickly as the cinnamon rolls he'd bought yesterday from the Daily Donut. Chase didn't begrudge his fourteen-year-old son, Wyatt, the opportunity to get burgers after school with his friends, but it only proved Wyatt's life had gone on without him. For the umpteenth time, Chase wished he hadn't wasted three precious years in prison.

All for his stupid pride.

He sighed then texted Wyatt to have fun and stay safe. This would be Chase's first Christmas in Lake Endwell, Michigan. He'd been living there for ten months, and as of last week, he'd successfully completed his parole. He was free. But free to do what? His former life as an NFL player was no longer an option, and he was too young not to have a job. The one thing he'd been considering probably wasn't even an option given his criminal record.

The doorbell rang. Must be Drew. Another person he'd desperately missed when serving his sentence. Chase could never repay his best friend, Drew Gannon, for raising Wyatt while he was in prison. He loped to the door, opened it wide. And did a double take.

Courtney?

Long, pale blond waves tumbled over her shoulders as snowflakes danced around her. Her dark blue eyes twinkled, and the white puffy jacket she wore hugged her slim body.

"Surprise?" She tilted her head to the side and opened her hands, but worry lurked in her expression.

Chase swallowed his shock. Courtney Trudesta had actually taken him up on his invitation. The widow of his former NFL teammate, JJ Trudesta, Courtney had faithfully written Chase letters every week while he was in prison and even after he'd gotten out. Her letters had been an anchor, a lifeline, a reminder he was more than a felon.

The letters had stopped coming a few months ago. He had no idea why. But after finding out from a mutual friend that Courtney's mother had died, Chase had called her, inviting her to spend the holidays in his guest cottage.

She'd declined.

He didn't blame her. What woman would want to be around him after the mistakes he'd made?

But here she was.

"Come in." He waved her inside. "What changed your mind?"

Several inches shorter than him, she shrugged, a soft smile playing on her lips. "A lot of things. Do you still have room for me?"

"Of course I have room." He winced. He'd forgotten about Treyvon. Drew and his wife, Lauren, had connected Treyvon with Chase a few years ago. Like Chase, Treyvon had been serving time, except the kid was in juvie. They'd shared their stories through letters. After Treyvon got released, he'd had nowhere to go. No way to support himself. No family or friends to turn to. Chase had taken him in. Treyvon was part of his family now.

"I'm imposing, aren't I?" Courtney took a step back, but Chase caught her hand, easing her inside.

"No, I have plenty of space. Three empty bedrooms. Each with a private bath. As for the guest cottage…remember how I told you about Treyvon Smith? He's home for Christmas break. He feels more comfortable having his own place, so I let him move into the guest cottage. I can ask him to bunk in one of the bedrooms, though. Then you can—"

"No, no, I couldn't ask you to do that." She shook her head, all that hair swishing. "I shouldn't have just shown up. I should have called."

He widened his stance, crossing his arms over his chest. "I have tons of room. And we won't be alone, if that's what you're worried about. Wyatt lives here, too, not that I've seen much of him lately. The kid is the busiest high school freshman I know."

Questions lurked in her eyes.

He wanted her to stay. She'd lost her husband JJ—a younger player Chase had taken under his wing—a few years ago. And now her mom. Shadows hung below her eyes. Probably wasn't sleeping well. He knew all about insomnia.

"Let me get your bags. You can rest, relax. Christmas is in two weeks. I don't want you alone for the holidays."

And he didn't want to be alone, either. Sure, he had Wyatt, Treyvon, Drew and the other friends he'd made in town. But none of them needed him right now.

Nobody needed him much at all anymore.

Courtney probably didn't either, but in case she did...

With every letter, she'd given him a ray of light. She'd treated him like Chase McGill, upstanding citizen and former NFL wide receiver, not Chase McGill, convicted felon of second degree attempted murder. He wasn't proud that he'd been trying to exact revenge on the man who'd killed Wyatt's mother. Every week, Courtney had made him forget for a few minutes that he'd made mistakes. Terrible mistakes.

And now he had a chance to make her forget, at least temporarily, that she'd lost the people most dear to her.

If anyone deserved a happy Christmas, it was Courtney.

He dropped his arms to his sides and looked into her eyes. "Come on, say you'll stay."

***

Why had she thought coming here was a good idea? Courtney blinked up at Chase. She'd forgotten how handsome he was. Sandy brown hair, square jaw, gray eyes, and a body chiseled from the gym. His black T-shirt showed off his muscular chest and biceps. She suppressed a sigh at all the male power standing before her.

Yes, she'd made a huge mistake.

"I'm sorry to put you on the spot, Chase." She turned to leave. "I'll just..."

"Oh no, you don't." He put his arm around her shoulders and whirled her into the foyer. "At least have a cup of coffee with me before you make up your mind."

The instant he touched her, the control over her do-the-right-thing side snapped. She'd driven three hours here for a reason. Leaving Chase's might be the polite move, but she had nowhere to go, no one to be with, and she'd never felt this lonely in her life.

If she could just get through the holidays…

"A cup of coffee would be great." She unwound her scarf. "Oh, wait. I forgot to mention…how do you feel about dogs?" Scrunching her nose, she waited for his reaction.

"Love 'em." He grinned.

"Do you mind if I bring in my teacup Yorkie?"

Scratching the slight stubble on his chin, he raised his eyebrows. "Sounds vicious."

"Boo Boo?" Her nerves vanished, and she laughed. "He's harmless."

Chase's smile ignited her pulse. "Bring him in."

"I'll go get him."

A minute later, she returned, carrying the two-pound dog.

"Are you sure he isn't a toy?" Chase took Boo Boo from her, cradling him to his chest, while Courtney took off her coat and boots. "You are a cute little thing, aren't you?" Boo Boo responded by trying to lick his face. Courtney followed Chase through the foyer.

"Wow, your home is beautiful." She couldn't get over how spacious and airy it was. A formal living room stood to her right and a formal dining to her left. Hardwood floors gleamed throughout. Chase led the way to the rear of the house, and she gasped at the sight of floor-to-ceiling windows with nonstop views of the lake, frozen over and topped with snow. A welcoming kitchen opened up to the enormous family room.

"I'm glad you like it. Sometimes it feels like a dream living here." He set Boo Boo on the floor and gestured for her to sit on a stool at the island. "How do you take your coffee?"

"Lots of cream and sugar."

He handed her a mug, sliding a small tray with cream and sugar her way, and took a seat across from her. She wasn't sure what to say, but maybe words weren't needed. The cozy atmosphere leaked the tension from her body.

"Before we catch up, I have to get this off my chest." He propped his elbows on the counter, clasping his hands. "Your letters...they kept me going. Thank you for taking the time to send them every week. You could have written me off...but you didn't. I can never repay you or thank you enough."

He thought all that? Her chest expanded.

"You don't have to thank me." She reached over and squeezed his hand. "If it hadn't been for you, JJ wouldn't have found the success he did. You were instrumental in his career. He looked up to you."

Chase nodded, his gaze faraway. "He was a brilliant player. He just needed someone to believe in him." He faced her again. "I'm sorry he died, Courtney. And I'm sorry you lost your mother, too."

She held her breath, afraid if she exhaled she'd start crying again and never stop. She was pretty sure she'd cried enough tears for a lifetime.

"Thanks, Chase. I appreciate it."

"I didn't deserve your support when I was in prison. I'm ashamed of what I did to be put there. I hurt my son. Killed my career. Let down my team. I don't blame you if you have reservations about staying here."

He didn't think she pitied him or saw him as a loser, did he? "I know you're sorry for what you did. To be honest, I understand why you did it."

The corner of his mouth lifted slightly. "You couldn't possibly know."

"I wanted the woman who hit JJ's car to pay, too." She straightened, toying with the handle of the coffee mug. "I fantasized about confronting her. Hurting her."

"But you didn't."

"No, but I wanted to."

"I wish I wouldn't have acted on my fantasies." He rapped his knuckles on the counter. "Oh, well. It's the price I'll have to bear."

"You paid the price." She took a small sip. Warm and delicious. "You can move on with your life."

He considered for a minute. Then he hitched his chin to her. "What about you? How are you moving on? I wish you weren't going through this."

Her throat tightened. She wasn't moving on. Not really. It was why she came. Get through the holidays without the constant reminders she was all alone in life. Then move to Indianapolis for a job in public relations that didn't excite her one bit. It had been several years since she'd worked, and taking care of her mom last year while she'd fought pancreatic cancer had depleted Courtney's emotional reserves.

The emptiness inside her howled.

"Courtney?"

"Hmm?"

"I wasn't saying it to be nice earlier. I want you to stay here for Christmas." His gray eyes gleamed with remorse, uncertainty and, most of all, kindness.

A girl could get lost in eyes like those.

Surely two weeks of not being alone wasn't too much to ask? Was it?

She swallowed, guilt tapping on the vault where she'd locked away her heart when JJ died. As long as she kept that vault sealed tight, Lake Endwell would give her a chance to get through Christmas before saying goodbye to her former life once and for all.

Chapter Two

Had he pushed her too hard? Chase studied Courtney, memorizing each detail. The dimples that flashed when she smiled. The way she fidgeted with her mug. The rigidness in her back. He got the impression she was as lost as he was, and he wanted her to find her way. If anyone should have a happy life, it was Courtney.

"Okay, you talked me into it." The dimples appeared momentarily. "But don't worry, I won't be in your way. Go about your business. Do what you do. You don't have to entertain me."

Chase frowned. *Do what you do?* If only she knew how at sea he'd become without the strict schedule of the NFL or the regiment of prison life. He couldn't remember a time when he'd had complete control over his days. Someone else had always spelled it out for him. Sure, he oversaw his business empire—the eleven sandwich franchises he owned and the investments from his NFL days—but his manager took care of most of the work.

What he wanted to do was start a program for kids like Treyvon who had nowhere to go after leaving juvenile detention. But who would listen to him given his record? Besides, he had no idea where to begin.

"You won't be in my way. Treyvon is busy helping organize a toy drive for one of the charities he joined on campus, and Wyatt's still in school until next week. Every afternoon I get a text saying he's sledding with Hunter or going to Pat's Diner with a bunch of friends."

She chuckled. "I remember those days. High school. Where the social opportunities never ended."

"Yeah, I remember them, too. I just wish..." He raked his fingers through his hair. "I feel like I missed the most important years with him. He's so busy. I had this big plan when I got out of prison. I was going to be the best dad ever. Devote all my time to him, you know?"

"I can see it." She nodded, raising the coffee cup for another drink.

"But his friends and girls and all the fun activities around here are way more of a draw than me."

She covered his hand with hers. It was the second time she'd touched him. He liked it. Hadn't ever had a woman comfort him with her touch before. Not his ornery mother. Certainly not Wyatt's mother, Missy.

"You're still important to him," she said.

He hoped so, but he had his doubts. "Look, I have nothing to complain about. I'm thankful the parole board released me early, and I'm fortunate to have all this." He opened his arms to the room. "I've wanted to live in Lake Endwell ever since I first met Drew Gannon—you remember him? My best friend? When we roomed together in college, he told me about his childhood here."

"I remember Drew. He was really nice." Boo Boo let out a yip, and Courtney reached down, setting the tiny dog on her lap. "You bought the house in February, right?"

"Good memory." He was surprised she remembered. A part of him had never quite believed she'd read the letters he wrote in response to hers.

"I have to admit, spending Christmas here at your lake house beats how I spent it last year." She picked a piece of fuzz off her pale pink sweater. A silver chain with a heart dangled from her neck. She was so…feminine and easy to talk to.

"Let's see. Last year you moved back in with your mom, right? Pittsburgh?"

Bowing her head, she nodded.

"Must have been really tough."

"It was. For months all I did was take her to chemo treatments and help her through the side effects. Last year we didn't even have a Christmas tree. It was awful."

"You did the right thing."

"I miss her," she whispered, clearly choked up. "And JJ."

"Me too. I don't know why God spared someone like me while allowing a good guy like JJ to die."

"You're a good guy, too, Chase." Her blue eyes seemed to stare right into his soul. Would she see that it was dirty and torn? Whatever she saw didn't seem to faze her based on her warm smile.

"Staying in Detroit last year instead of coming here to spend Christmas with Wyatt was one of the hardest things I've done." A year ago he'd been released from prison early and put on parole, but he hadn't driven straight to Lake

Endwell. After discussing the situation with Drew and Wyatt, he'd spent over a month in Detroit. Due to his celebrity status, tabloids and television crews had followed his case from day one. As soon as he was released, a media circus had descended on him. Chase refused all interviews and ignored the press, but it had taken weeks for them to leave him alone. He hadn't wanted Wyatt in the center of all the hoopla. Before Chase had been convicted, photographers had harassed the kid for months. So he'd stayed away. And it had been so, so difficult.

"It was wise of you." Her eyes radiated kindness. "You honored your promise to Wyatt. No unnecessary media attention."

"You remembered." She really had read his letters.

"Why do you sound so surprised? I thought it was wise to put Wyatt's needs first."

He ambled across the room to stand near the windows overlooking the white lake. Courtney followed him. He shoved his hands in his pockets. "I honestly never thought giving the interview to People Magazine while I was in prison would hurt and embarrass Wyatt the way it did." He turned to face her. "I'm a self-absorbed jerk."

"You're not a jerk." She took a seat in one of his oversized leather chairs. "All you football players were used to reporters and the celebrity craziness. You didn't realize it would affect Wyatt."

"I do now. No interviews or publicity. I will never hurt Wyatt like that again."

"I know." She tried to hide her yawn.

Here he was going on and on about himself, and she was practically falling asleep from exhaustion. He'd better settle her into a room and let her get some rest.

"Well, Courtney, this year we're going to make up for last year's rotten Christmas. While I get your bags, you can pick out your room."

He finally had a chance to repay her for her kindness. Courtney didn't know it yet, but he was going to take care of her for a change, the way she'd taken care of JJ and her mom. Maybe they both needed this Christmas to recover from their pasts.

***

She could restore her soul in a room like this. Courtney's head fell into the fluffy pillow, and she clasped her hands on her stomach as she lay on top of the down comforter. The décor was all whites and pale blues. It reminded her of the ocean. Chase had brought her suitcases up a few minutes ago, and Boo Boo had sniffed every corner of the room before she'd hauled him onto the bed with her. He'd promptly curled into a ball and fallen asleep.

Lord, thank You for pushing me to come here. This is the first time I've felt a glimmer of hope in months.

Chase's humility added an interesting element to her impression of him. She remembered him being take charge, sure of himself, and very generous. When JJ struggled his rookie season, it was Chase who had taken him under his wing, given him advice, included him in his daily routine and made sure he stayed positive. Chase had also invited JJ and her to gatherings at his house with the rest of the team and their wives. She'd always found it curious such a handsome, charismatic guy had never married.

She hadn't known about his past with Missy at the time, but JJ had told her the story. Chase and Missy had dated in college. Then Missy got pregnant, and Chase was drafted to Chicago. They had the baby, spent two years in Illinois, but when Chase got traded to Detroit, he and Missy had broken up. She'd gotten involved with a drug-dealer named Len and had become an addict herself. Somewhere in there Chase gained custody of Wyatt. In recent years Missy had completed rehab and moved to Detroit. She and Chase had started dating again before Len tracked her down and murdered her.

Courtney frowned, sad over a woman she'd never met and for what it had done to Chase. He'd snapped. Went after Len. Ran him over with his truck. Broke the guy's leg and was charged with attempted murder. Both men went to jail. Chase had been sentenced to six years but got out early. Len was completing a life sentence.

Courtney's eyelids grew heavy. Poor Chase. He seemed mired in remorse, but he'd paid for his crime. Didn't he see it shouldn't define him?

Who was she to talk? JJ's death defined her. She'd tiptoed through life ever since losing him. The only thing that had gotten her moving was her mom's illness.

But Mom was gone, too. And the past months of listlessness had vanished when Chase called, inviting her here for the holidays. Initially she'd declined. Sure, they were friends. But was mere friendship with a gorgeous, single, charismatic man even possible?

Really, Courtney? You don't have to worry about anything beyond friendship. He's Chase McGill. You're his friend's wife. Well, you were, anyway.

She cringed. Who was she if she was no longer JJ Trudesta's wife?

As usual, she was overthinking things.

She had a two-week reprieve from a future she didn't really want. Spending the holidays with Chase McGill was the escape she needed.

CHAPTER THREE

The last time he'd eaten dinner with a woman had been…with Missy. The night before she'd died. Chase pulled Chinese takeout containers from the delivery bag. He hadn't seen Courtney since dropping off her luggage to the room she'd picked out two hours prior. Hopefully, she was sleeping. She'd tried to hide her weariness, but anyone could see she'd been dead on her feet. In the meantime, his thoughts kept going back to Wyatt's mother.

He could think about Missy now without getting choked up. He attributed it to his faith. God had forgiven him for his many errors when it came to her. Chase hadn't been a believer when they'd met. The day he'd found out Missy was a drug addict was when he'd dropped down to his knees and admitted he needed a Savior. A clean soul in place of his filthy past. He'd fought for custody of his precious young son and won. That had been a decade ago.

He'd put his trust in God and never looked back. Tried to live a Christian life and be a light to those around him. And he'd succeeded…until he went after Len.

"Hey, what smells so good?" Courtney rounded the corner. Her hair was tousled and her cheeks pink. She took his breath away.

"You like Chinese?" He gestured to the food. His entertaining skills were rusty. Or maybe the fact a beautiful woman would be eating with him was making him nervous.

"Yep." She reached across him for a plate, her light perfume lingering.

He stilled. What was he doing? He couldn't think of her in a romantic way. This was JJ's widow, for crying out loud!

He busied himself finding a playlist of the Rat Pack. The lively music crooned from the speakers. Some twinkly lights would go a long way to making the dark house feel more festive. He'd have to decorate it soon.

"Where have you been living?" Chase filled a plate and sat across from Courtney at the table in the eat-in kitchen.

"After I sold Mom's house I moved back to Royal Oak, but it was impossible. Too big. Too empty without JJ. I sold that house, too."

He'd been to her and JJ's home before. It had a woman's touch. He'd always felt welcome there.

"Where will you live now?" he asked.

"Indianapolis." She took a bite of lo mein. "I got a job in public relations. I start in January. I'm nervous about it. I haven't had a job in seven years. You know how it was as an NFL wife."

He did. "It's a job in itself. Keeping track of everything— the schedule, travel, bills, the off season. I always admired you for that."

Her cheeks flushed. "At least the last job I had was in public relations as well. Shouldn't be too much of a stretch."

"But?" He liked watching her talk. She had a demure quality he found refreshing.

"I don't know. Nothing excites me lately."

"You'll get there and love it. Just takes a while to adjust. I know what you mean about nothing exciting you, though. Whenever I try to figure out what I'm supposed to do with myself, I get lost. Well, that's not entirely true. I have this idea—it won't stop bugging me—but the least of my problems is not knowing where to begin. I'll stick to owning my franchises and call it good."

"What's the idea?" She tilted her head, a spring roll dripping with sauce poised between her fingers.

"It's hard to explain." He shuffled the sweet and sour chicken around on his plate. "You know how Treyvon and I started writing to each other while I was in prison? Well, it was because of Drew's wife Lauren. Drew told me about the kid's situation, and I couldn't get him out of my mind. I wrote to him. He wrote back. And we both had this huge burden of guilt, but we also knew God had forgiven us. It was eerie how much we had in common. But Treyvon had none of the things I could rely on—no family or friends, no money. As time passed, I wanted to change that. He worked hard while he was in juvie. Got his high school diploma. Good grades, too. I told him he would always have a home with Wyatt and me. And now he goes to Western Michigan University. Studying to be a lawyer."

"Good for him. You should be proud of yourself, Chase. You gave him direction."

"Nah," he shook his head, "It was all him. It got me thinking, though, about how many kids age out of the juvenile detention system and, like Treyvon, have nowhere to turn. No money. No place to live. Can you imagine?"

She blinked. "No, I can't. I've never thought about it. How awful."

"I agree. So I have this idea to start a program for kids like him. Get them financial support, a place to live, a group of mentors to help them stay out of trouble."

"What a great idea!" She set her fork down and clasped her hands together.

Chase couldn't stop staring at her. *Have mercy.* "Yeah, well, it's just a bunch of thoughts in my head at this point."

"This could change their lives. Put those thoughts together. You're on to something."

Him, change lives? Doubtful. But hearing her say it? Made him want to listen to her for hours on end. "Like I said, I don't have much at this point."

Once again, her blue eyes seemed to see right into his soul.

Courtney Trudesta was the most alluring woman he'd ever met.

He couldn't have her.

Couldn't even think about having her.

A woman like Courtney was entitled to a stand-up guy. Not an ex-felon like him.

***

"Why don't you tell me more about it?" Courtney didn't like the way Chase had clammed up a minute ago. A program to help eighteen-year-olds fresh out of juvenile hall was inspiring. Surely, he knew that.

"I feel like it's too big." Chase had a strange look in his eye. Like the Chinese food had hit him wrong. The man wasn't going to vomit, was he?

"Are you feeling okay?" She touched his hand. He practically jumped out of his skin.

"I'm good." He gulped down his water. "There are so many factors to get into place. Maybe I'm fooling myself. Who am I to start something like that?"

Didn't the man have a clue how many people he'd helped over the years? Still helped?

"It is big. There are a lot of factors. But it doesn't mean it can't be done. I serve on several charity boards. You just have to take it step by step."

He met her eyes, and she momentarily forgot the conversation, their surroundings. It was like spiraling into a world where she instinctively belonged but had never stepped foot into before.

She averted her gaze, preoccupying herself with her food. She hadn't come here to get romantic with Chase. This was only a blip of attraction, right?

She'd vowed to love, honor, and cherish JJ, and she had. Until she'd lost him.

Had she lost herself, too?

She was too empty to give Chase what he needed—a woman brimming with vibrancy.

The door to the garage opened and a tall teen walked in. He set his backpack on the floor and stopped short when he saw Courtney. She tried to remember the last time she'd seen Wyatt. He'd probably been about nine years old. Cute. Fresh-faced. He was still adorable.

"Wyatt, this is Courtney Trudesta. I don't know if you remember her. JJ and I played football together. She's spending the holidays with us."

She steeled herself for his reaction. She hadn't thought about how her presence would affect Chase's son. But to her relief, he grinned and walked over.

"Nice to meet you." Wyatt stuck his hand out. "You wrote Dad all the letters, right?"

"I did." She couldn't help but smile as she shook his hand. "I hope you don't mind me staying here. I'll keep out of your way."

"I don't mind. I hope you don't stay out of the way. Dad and I could use help in the Christmas department. We don't even have a tree. And I need to go shopping for presents."

Chase cocked his head. "It's true. We're unprepared."

"I want to get Briana something special." Wyatt grabbed a plate and dumped half the food on it.

"Wait, who's Brianna?" Chase turned to face him.

"Hunter's girlfriend's best friend. We've been talking."

Chase met Courtney's eyes. She almost laughed. He looked way out of his element.

"What is she interested in?" she asked.

He shrugged, shoveling a mouthful of rice into his mouth as he joined them at the table.

"Does she wear jewelry?" Courtney could list any number of items a teen girl would love.

"Yeah."

"Gold? Silver? Colorful stuff?"

"Hmm…silver. Nothing real big, though."

"Maybe you should get her a necklace."

"Good idea." He snapped his fingers, addressing Chase. "Can I get an advance on my allowance? I want to buy it this weekend."

"You know what's on your chore list. I'll give you your allowance when you finish it."

"Aw, Dad." Wyatt groaned. "I hate cleaning the bathroom."

"No one likes it." Chase winked at Courtney. Warmth spread up from her toes to her head. It was fun listening to their banter. Made her wonder…what would life be like if JJ hadn't died? Would she have children?

She swirled her fork into her noodles. That line of thought would only get her into trouble.

"So Courtney, you said you served on charity boards," Chase said. "Do you have any advice for me about the juvenile program?"

"Write down your objectives. Brainstorm what you'll need to meet them. Research the plausibility—how likely is it for your program to succeed? You'll need to prove its worth to investors or sponsors. Come up with a business plan. Then start finding the money to make it happen." She rattled off the list with ease. She knew exactly what he needed to do. She'd been doing it for years.

He gulped. Funny, seeing a strong, take-charge guy like Chase nervous. Didn't seem possible.

"Your plan is worth pursuing, Chase."

He scratched his neck, clearly not believing her.

"I'll be here for a few weeks," she said. "I'll help you get started."

As soon as she said it, she wondered if it was wise. But the look of gratitude Chase gave her evaporated her worries. His idea was something she could get behind. And she wanted to help him. The way he was helping her. Besides, how many nights had she eaten dinner alone? For months and months. Sharing a meal with these two made her feel alive again.

Yes, giving Chase a few business tips was a small way to repay his kindness. It would be a relief to feel useful for once. She had a two-week reprieve from a future she didn't really want. Spending the holidays with Chase McGill was the escape she needed.

Chapter Four

While Wyatt was in school, Chase decided to show Courtney around Lake Endwell the next morning. Would she see its charm? Fall in love with it the way he had? He opened the door of the coffee shop and followed her outside, a to-go cup in hand. The sun was out, an inch of snow covered the bushes and trees, and everywhere he looked wreaths and red bows hung from doors and light posts. "Let me know if you want to duck into any of the stores."

"I will. This might be the cutest town in Michigan." Holding a takeout cup in her mitten covered hands, Courtney strolled next to Chase. "I can't believe I've never been here. How do you like living on the lake?"

"Love it." He glanced at her. Her words put an extra bounce in his step. They passed a jewelry store and the pizza joint. "Best decision I've made. The people here are nice, Wyatt's happy, and my best friend lives a mile away."

"Sounds as though you fit right in."

As if to prove her point, someone called, "Hey, Chase!" On the other side of the street, Tom Sheffield, loaded with packages, walked toward them. The Sheffield family was very active in Lake Endwell. They'd welcomed him with open arms. They had no idea how much their acceptance meant to him.

"Hey, Tom," he replied, waving.

"You're coming to our party, right? Next week Wednesday. The night before Christmas eve."

"Sure am."

"Bring your friend." Tom grinned and tossed his packages into a white truck.

"Who was that?" Courtney asked.

"Oh, that's Tom Sheffield. He owns a car dealership outside of town. The Sheffields are a big part of Lake Endwell." They kept walking. He couldn't get over how easy she was to be with—slim and cute and...

"How many Sheffields are there?" She sipped her coffee, glancing up at him with those big blue eyes.

"Let's see." He squinted, trying to keep them straight. "Tom, Bryan, Sam—the three brothers run the dealerships of Sheffield Auto—then there's Claire and Libby. They're the sisters. They're all married. All have kids. I think Bryan's wife, Jade, is pregnant again. Maybe Libby, too. I can't keep track. Jade and Libby own Shine Gifts down the street. Dale is the Sheffield patriarch. His sister Sally's husband Joe owns my favorite restaurant in town—Uncle Joe's Restaurant. I'll take you there sometime."

"I will never in a million years keep all that straight."

He laughed. "When you meet them, it will all make sense."

"I'm not surprised you fit right in." Her breath spiraled in the cold air. "You always had a knack for social connections."

Did he fit in, though? The Sheffields treated him like they did everyone else, but some people in town avoided him. He didn't blame them. Who wanted an ex-convict in their neighborhood?

They reached the end of the street. He pointed ahead where a paved bike trail wound past the town Christmas tree before edging around the lake. "Want to keep going? The gazebo has a great view."

"Sure." She tossed her cup in the trash bin.

The chilly air nipped at his cheeks. He stole a peek at Courtney. She had a serene expression on her face and easily kept pace with him.

"Just think, two years ago you and I were about as low as we could be." She flashed him a bright smile. "And here we are enjoying a winter's day. Hard to believe life has changed so much."

"It's good to see you enjoying this." Maybe he shouldn't have said that out loud. He cleared his throat. "Two years ago, I could barely imagine life out of prison. I kept all of your letters. On hard days, I would reread them." They stopped in front of a large evergreen strung with ornaments and lights. Benches surrounded it.

"Want to sit a minute?" He brushed snow off the nearest bench.

"You really kept my letters? I'm embarrassed to think of all I put in them. I was so vulnerable. I hope I didn't make a fool of myself."

He shifted to look at her. "You could never make a fool of yourself. Not with me. Your letters kept me going."

She lowered her eyelashes. "After JJ died, no one knew what to do with me. The players and wives stopped by now and then, but after a few months, I was alone. I think they grew uncomfortable. I didn't know what to do or say. All I knew was life as I knew it was over."

He took her hand in his. "Mine was too. But reading about your days helped…I laughed so hard over the hot pad incident."

She grinned, chuckling. "I forgot about that! Oh, I was a mess. How did I manage to set the hot pads on fire? I was just taking chicken out of the oven."

"And you forgot the burner was on for the potatoes."

"Poof!" She made an exploding gesture with her hands.

"I was relieved you weren't burned." He enjoyed her animation when she talked. Those dimples popped out. Her eyes danced. In her letters, Courtney was self-deprecating, witty, and real. In person, she was dynamic, intriguing…tempting.

"I looked forward to your letters, too, Chase. You made me feel normal when my life was anything but. I'm impressed with your devotion to Wyatt."

"I let Wyatt down." He squirmed. "I don't ever want to let him down again."

"We're human. We let people down sometimes."

He shifted to face her. "I don't believe you've ever let anyone down."

"I have." She shook her head. "I will again. And you will, too. It's part of life."

She was right, but it bothered him. He wanted to be better. Wanted to live up to his own expectations. Wanted to be the hero he used to be. *What a joke.* He was too tarnished. He'd made too many mistakes.

"I can't get over all the books you read." Courtney shivered, rubbing her hands together.

"I was doing my best to get through each day."

"Well, a lot of people get through by blaming everyone else and sitting around. You took responsibility, made the most of your time there, and helped other people."

Praise? From her? He had to set her straight. She thought he was someone he wasn't. "I'm nothing great. I will always carry the label of felon."

"And I'll always carry the label of widow."

***

"You haven't gotten over him, have you?" Chase asked quietly. His words held no judgment. Just sympathy. Understanding.

"I should have by now. I know it." A lump formed in her throat. It had been over three years since the accident. Three long years alone, without the man who'd stolen her heart and made her certain she belonged right there by his side. Even when he was on the road for a game or at training camp, she'd felt secure in her identity as JJ's wife.

"I'm not an expert on this stuff by any means. Frankly, I'm the last person to talk. But what you and JJ had was real. We all saw it. All knew it. A love like yours…most of us would have given our right eye for it. I don't blame you for not getting over him. JJ was solid. Everyone loved him."

Tears pressed against her eyes. "Thank you." She willed her emotions away. She'd cried enough for JJ and for her mother. If she never cried again, she still would have cried enough. "You must have loved Missy the same."

His eyes darkened to slate. "If you would have said that to me after she was murdered, I would have agreed."

"Why am I sensing a *but*?" She hadn't meant to bring up a painful subject. She'd assumed...

"I didn't know what real love was. I went after Len because I was angry. Yes, I was upset and sad Missy was dead. But she and I had a dysfunctional relationship from day one. What we had was nothing like what you had with JJ." Chase stood, holding his hand out. She let him help her up. "You're cold. Come on, let's go someplace warm."

Before she lost her nerve, she twined her arms around his back and gave him a hug. No one had cared or even noticed if she was cold or warm in so long, she'd forgotten what it was like to have someone notice, let alone care.

He pulled her close to him, holding her gently. "I'm sorry you lost him, Courtney."

Resting her cheek against the fleece of his jacket, she could hear his heartbeat through the material. Strong. Like him. His embrace reminded her of sinking into a hot bath after a long day.

"Thank you." She eased back to stare into his eyes. "For reaching out, for inviting me to stay. I've been pretty low. Lost, really. Being here with you, well, it makes me believe I might be okay."

"Stay as long as you want. You're always welcome here. If it hadn't been for your letters..." His gaze held an intensity, a loneliness she recognized. Her pulse sped up.

Don't get caught up in sugarplums and Christmas wishes, Court. Lake Endwell isn't forever. You have a job waiting for you.

For a moment, she wanted it to last forever. She'd never dreamed spending less than twenty-four hours with Chase would cement the friendship they'd nurtured for almost four years.

Friendship was one thing. How she was reacting to an innocent embrace was another.

"I appreciate it, but I'll be moving soon." She stepped back, pasting her brightest smile on. His slow nod held resignation. "I think it's time for me to get a life."

Chapter Five

"This can't be right. Have you ever cut one of these down before, Dad?"

Chase grunted then shifted to the side and stared up from under the Christmas tree he was attempting to cut down. The smell of pine trees and freshly cut bark filled the air. "What do you mean? I've got the saw. We picked out the tree. What more am I supposed to be doing?"

"I'm a hundred percent positive you're cutting it wrong." Wyatt looked disgusted as he turned to Courtney, who appeared ready to burst into laughter as she stomped her boots to stay warm. "Does this look right to you?"

Even from this angle, Chase could see her eyes sparkling. He fought back a groan. From the instant she stepped into his arms earlier, he'd been fighting a losing battle.

He was attracted to her.

Not just physically. Emotionally, mentally—every way a man could be attracted to a woman. Hearing her say his letters had meant something to her had rocked his world. Then when she'd praised him for his devotion to Wyatt, for reading books, for helping people? His heart couldn't take it. What would a class act like her want with a dumb jock who'd taken the law into his hands and gone to prison?

But she made it sound as if his letters had helped her. That she appreciated them. And, more, she still seemed to appreciate him. What she'd revealed about losing her football family had been sobering.

How lonely had the past couple of years been for her?

The one question he didn't even want to think kept pressing into his brain.

Why had she stopped writing?

He couldn't bear to ask. Wasn't ready for her answer.

"Dad, you're supposed to cut off those low branches so you can have a clear shot at the trunk." Wyatt scrolled through his phone. "It says so right here."

"If you're such an expert, why don't you get down here in the snow and do it?" He held the saw up.

Wyatt backed up a step with his hands at his chest. "Oh, no. That's all you."

"Do you boys need me to take over?" Courtney's teeth gleamed she was smiling so big. Actually, he wouldn't mind seeing her cute little body shimmy under the tree…

"Nope. Got it." He slid back under and did as Wyatt suggested. Lopped off the small lower branches and got to work on the main trunk. Soon, the blue spruce toppled over, and he jumped up, brushing the snow, dirt, and needles off his clothes. "There."

"I'll take it to the tree shaker." Wyatt grabbed it by the trunk and began dragging it through the lane. Chase and Courtney fell in behind him. The kid was fast, though, and quickly outdistanced them.

"You two seem to be getting along well," Courtney said. "I remember for a while there, he wasn't talking to you. It was early into your sentence. Then things slowly got better between you."

Chase stole a peek at her. Pink nose from the cold temperature. Black snow boots. Tight jeans. Her puffy jacket. Blond hair flowing down her back. This stunning woman really had paid attention to his life.

"We're doing okay. It took a while for us to find our groove. I think the biggest thing is having no secrets. If he's mad at me, he tells me. I make the rules, but I talk to Drew and Lauren if I'm worried I'm being too tough. They're still a huge part of his life. I don't know what I would have done without them."

"I think you're being wise."

"When I got out on parole, I made him my number one priority."

"I was glad when you wrote and told me you'd decided to stay in Detroit for a while after your release. The media can be relentless. You're a good father."

Was he a good father? He tried to be, but his expectations didn't always line up with reality.

"He's growing up. I guess when I got out I thought he'd still be a ten-year-old kid who'd want to hang out with his dad."

She nodded. "But instead you got a popular teenager who wants to hang out with his friends."

He stopped walking. She did, too.

"That's it exactly." He shook his head. "And in a few years, he'll be in college."

"You'll be on your own." She nudged his arm for them to keep walking. They moved forward. "I guess it's time for you to get a life, too."

"I guess it is." And he didn't like it. Wanted his life to be neat and orderly. It felt too wide open.

Wyatt stood at the end of the lane. "Come on guys, what's taking you so long?"

Chase rolled his eyes. Courtney laughed. "Shall we?"

They jogged ahead, catching up to Wyatt. Chase wrapped his arm around Wyatt's neck. "You telling me I'm a slowpoke, son?"

"I am." Wyatt laughed. "Don't try and deny it."

"Let's get this tree home and decorate it." He pulled Wyatt into a half embrace. Wyatt slung his arm around Chase's back and grinned up at him.

He might have to get a life like Courtney said, but in the meantime, he'd savor every moment with Wyatt. And with her.

***

Courtney had been fighting the warm fuzzies all day, and watching Chase and Wyatt interact—having them treat her as if she belonged here—had left her ridiculously happy but nervous just the same. She couldn't simply show up at their house and be part of their family. It didn't work that way.

"Are we ordering pizza?" Wyatt dropped another bin of Christmas decorations on the family room floor with a thud.

"I'll cook." She wanted to do something nice for them. She mentally ticked through her favorite meals.

Chase was on his knees, trying to get the tree to stay straight in its stand. Boo Boo sat right next to his head, watching him intently. Sliding out from under the tree, he stood, surveying it. "You're our guest. You don't have to cook. Maybe I need to duct tape this."

"Yeah, we have pizza three times a week," Wyatt said, waving dismissively. "It's no big deal."

"I want to make you a meal." She'd always loved to cook. She just didn't enjoy making dinner for one. "I really appreciate you letting me stay with you. How does lasagna sound?"

"Lasagna? Mm-mm. My favorite." Wyatt rubbed his stomach. "Dad, the tree is beyond crooked."

The side door opened and a low male voice hollered, "You guys home?"

"Treyvon!" Wyatt loped over to him and bumped fists. "How did the thing go today?"

"The thing? You mean the toy drive." His tone was all teasing. "All the presents are delivered, and I'm officially off duty until the new year." Treyvon stepped into the family room. Whew, he was tall. Six three at least. Dark skinned and handsome. He wore a light gray sweatshirt and dark jeans. When he noticed her, he hitched his chin. "Hey, what's up? I'm Treyvon Smith."

"Hi, Treyvon." She closed the distance and held out her hand. He shook it. "Courtney Trudesta."

His eyes widened. "You're Courtney? Man, it is an honor to meet you. Chase told me how you wrote him every week. Not many people do that, you know. You're one special lady."

Her neck grew warm, and she was positive her cheeks were flaming. "It was the least I could do. Chase was a good friend to my late husband."

"Yeah, sorry about your loss. He sure could play ball."

Usually when someone expressed their sympathies, she got choked up. But this time she simply nodded. Maybe she was starting to move on. She hoped so. Or was it dishonoring JJ's memory to not feel sad whenever he came up?

"Do you like lasagna, Treyvon?"

"I love it."

"Lasagna it is." She zipped her jacket and slung her purse over her shoulder. "I'll head to the store. I saw a market outside town."

"Lake Endwell Grocery." Chase must have finished with the tree because he'd zoomed next to her with Boo Boo in his arms. He was petting the dog. Her heart flip-flopped. "I'll come with you."

"No, no." She needed air. Alone. Nowhere near this gorgeous guy who wasn't too manly to carry around her tiny dog. "I'll find it. Be right back."

"Are you sure?" He narrowed his eyes.

She nodded brightly.

"Well, Boo Boo, let's get those lights strung while your mommy goes shopping." His tone was so sweet she instantly pictured him cradling a baby.

Babies. What she'd wanted more than anything. And JJ had kept asking her to wait. *Wait until we get through this season. Wait until I sign a long-term contract. Wait, wait, wait.*

She looked around at the three guys in the room, all of whom towered over her. Chase had his family. They were all grown up.

She'd never gotten hers.

If Chase met someone, would he want more babies?

Someone? You mean you, Courtney. Stop playing with temptation.

She hurried to the door.

"Have you ever decorated a tree before?" Wyatt's voice carried. "That's not how you string lights."

"Boy, you know everything, don't you? As a matter of fact, I haven't ever decorated one before. I always hired someone to do it..."

Being with Chase and his family was easy. Too easy. But if she got too close, it would be worse than hard to lose them. It would be devastating. She'd lost too much already.

Chapter Six

Chase stood on the deck and looked out over frozen Lake Endwell. The sun was rising. Snow drifted along the shore. Down the way a large section had been shoveled for a makeshift ice rink. He never tired of this view. Didn't matter the season the lake fascinated him.

And the woman sleeping upstairs in his guest room? Fascinated him, too.

Spending the past couple of days with her had filled a hole he hadn't realized was there. Every day after Wyatt left for school, Chase and Courtney would start talking and not stop until they realized it was lunchtime. He'd taken her to Pat's Diner yesterday for a down home meal. Afterward, they'd come back here. Courtney had played Christmas music through his sound system, and they'd fallen into another conversation lasting for hours.

He'd learned she'd graduated from Penn State, where she'd met JJ, and they'd gotten married the summer before his rookie season in Detroit. She had no siblings. Her dad died when she was young, and she and her mother had been close. Losing her had crushed her.

Other things—unspoken things—had come through loud and clear. She was struggling to fit in without having JJ and her mother anymore. The thought of reentering the workforce intimidated her. He got the impression she had no idea what an amazing person she was.

He wanted her to know. Didn't want any confusion on her part that she was special. The most incredible woman he'd ever met.

"Mind if I join you?"

He whirled, almost spilling his coffee. Courtney's hair was pulled back in a ponytail, and her face was free of makeup. She wore gray sweatpants and a light pink sweatshirt, and her feet were tucked into fuzzy boots. Steam from the mug she carried drifted to the sky.

"I love this view." He shifted as she stood next to him. "You should see it in the summer. And the fall."

Her smile teased. "Not the spring?"

"Oh, definitely see it in the spring." He tried not to stare but without makeup she seemed even prettier than usual.

"I feel like I'm in another world here." Her hands cradled the mug.

"I do, too. It's a world I only dreamed about. Drew used to tell me stories of growing up in this town, and I thought it must be the best place in the entire world."

"And now what do you think?"

"I was right. It's the best place in the entire world."

"Where did you grow up?" She took a tentative drink. "Mm...this is good."

"Trailer park in Texas. Dad left before I could walk. Mom did her best, but she was young. Worked two jobs, partied to blow off steam. I didn't have much structure as a kid. Thankfully, I found it in football."

"Really? And yet you're so driven." She looked taken aback. "Interesting."

"What do you mean?" He rested his elbow on the deck rail.

"Structure is important to you."

He nodded. "Yeah. It is. That's why moving here...well, it's been great, but it's been a struggle in some ways as well."

"Ah."

"What?"

"We both have too much time on our hands with no real clue what to do with it."

Exactly.

She turned to face him, and he couldn't help adding up the fact mere inches separated them and she smelled like vanilla and flowers. A combination which shouldn't be enticing, and yet, was.

"I know what we're going to do today." She tapped her index finger against his chest. He forgot how to breathe.

"You do?" His voice was husky.

"Yep." She beamed. "We're going to brainstorm your idea about supporting kids getting out of the juvenile detention system."

Hope flickered but his conscience blew it out. Dare he believe he'd be able to start the program? "That's okay. You're here to relax and enjoy the holidays."

"I can relax and brainstorm at the same time." Her eyes challenged him. "I need a project. Come on, let's do this."

"Shouldn't we be doing things fun for you? I feel bad. This shouldn't be all about me."

She placed her free hand on her hip. "This isn't all about you. It's about me. Did you ever stop and think maybe I want to show off all the mad skills I picked up on the boards of those charities?"

He chuckled. She sure was cute. He wanted to reach out and touch her hair, slide his hand around her waist, tug her to him, and bring his lips to hers.

Slow down. You can't kiss her!

This was Courtney. Off limits.

For a cold day, it sure felt hot.

"Then don't let me stop you." He waved toward the house. "Show me those mad skills of yours."

***

Three hours later, Courtney rubbed her eyes. She hadn't felt this alive in...she couldn't remember when. As she stretched her arms over her head, the legal pad in her lap slipped to the carpet. She and Chase had started volleying ideas at the kitchen table. Then they'd moved into the family room and turned on the Christmas tree lights. They'd nibbled on pastries as they talked. Happiness bubbled up inside her. She wanted to wrap her arms around this day and never let it go.

"Okay, so we know the ideal candidates for the program." He tapped his pen against his thigh. "Eighteen years old. No good situation to return to. They need places to live, job references, financial aid, and mentors. Mentors are the big thing. Don't want them resuming a bad way of life."

"Based on what you've told me, I think you'll have to start small. One city. If it's successful, you can expand it."

"I think you're right. I'll see which cities in Michigan have juvenile centers." He began typing on his laptop.

She studied him. Eyebrows furrowed, pen tucked behind his ear, long-sleeved tee stretching across his chest—he meant business. He circled his neck back, shrugging his shoulders one at a time. She had the craziest urge to climb onto the couch next to him and massage his back. She'd done it for JJ a million times.

But Chase wasn't her husband.

She forced herself to concentrate on her notes.

"The closest detention center is an hour away." He looked up from the screen. "That's not too bad. We could start there."

We? She liked the sound of that much more than she should.

"How would the financing work, though?" He set the laptop to the side.

"This is a nonprofit, right?"

"Yeah. I don't need money. Between my NFL earnings, investments, and my franchises, I'm set for life."

Didn't surprise her. She was set for life, too. Her husband had earned a lot of money in the NFL, his life insurance had been astronomical, and she'd inherited her mother's estate.

"I'm assuming you'd be setting up a 501(c)(3). You'll need a mission statement, business plan, and a board of directors. Make an appointment with your lawyer."

They both scratched notes on their pads.

"Courtney?"

"What?"

"Do you think *I* could be a mentor?" The anguish in his eyes surprised her.

"Why not?" She set her papers down.

"I want to help these kids, but...I'm worried." He rubbed his chin. "What if I'm disqualified? Because I'm a convicted felon?"

She hadn't thought of that. "I don't know, Chase. When these kids get out, they're legal adults. I don't know the laws, but I would think they would listen to you more because you've been there. Plus, they would look up to you, given the fact you were a much-loved NFL star."

He still looked concerned. She got up and sat next to him on the couch. Took his hand in hers. "Who mentors alcoholics in alcoholics anonymous?"

"Former alcoholics."

"So who better to mentor someone in this situation than you?"

He slumped and his chin dropped. He pinched the bridge of his nose.

"I've made so many mistakes." He looked up, regrets swimming in his eyes. "Who am I to think I can help someone?"

Her heart ached for him, and she searched for the right thing to say. *Lord, Chase needs You. Will You show him how wonderful he is? How much a difference he makes in people's lives?*

She put her arm around his back, placing her cheek against his shoulder. "Moses murdered someone, and God used him to lead the Israelites out of Egypt."

"But that was Moses."

"And David had Bathsheba's husband killed. Don't forget it."

"But that was David."

"And you're you. God has plans for you, Chase. Don't let regrets keep you from your destiny."

He drew her into a hug. "Thank you. You have no idea how much you've helped me over the years. I'm glad you're here."

Her throat tightened. He was glad she was here? She'd helped him? Didn't he have it backward?

"You're the one who is helping me, Chase. The thought of spending Christmas alone..." She shook her head. This man didn't know she'd barely been able to get out of bed two months ago.

How was she ever going to leave when Christmas was over?

"Come on." She uncurled her legs. "We've been at this for hours. We need a break. What screams Christmas to you?"

"The Christmas Eve football game." Grinning, he rose.

She rolled her eyes. "Okay, besides that."

He thought about it a minute. "Buying presents. Attempting to wrap the presents. And eating a ton of Christmas cookies."

"Are you up for shopping?" she asked.

He looked queasy.

"Cookies it is."

CHAPTER SEVEN

"This way." Chase pressed his hand against Courtney's lower back to guide her into the pew Sunday morning. Her cream blouse and black skirt were conservative but showed off her trim figure to perfection. She oozed class.

Wyatt and Treyvon shuffled in next to them. Poinsettias lined the front of the sanctuary, and two tall Christmas trees twinkled up there, too. Piano music played as people quietly found seats. All morning he'd been wired and tense. Spending all this time with Courtney had been like nothing he'd ever experienced. He'd never gotten so close to a woman, never shared his emotions and hopes. Not even with Missy. But Courtney had loosened something inside him.

Lord, I think I'm falling for her. I can't. I know it's wrong. I promised to keep Wyatt my number one priority. And I've only been out of prison a year. Plus, this is the widow of my old teammate—a man I considered a good friend. I can't dishonor his memory like that. Oh, who am I fooling? She'd never be interested in me anyhow.

Courtney flipped through the pages of the service and leaned in close to him. "It's been months since I've attended church."

"Really?" He kept his voice low. "I hope I didn't pressure you into it. If you're uncomfortable…"

She placed her hand on his sleeve. He liked the feel of it there. "You didn't. Your church is serene. It's exactly what I need right now."

The service began, and Chase willed himself to focus. Succeeded for the most part. The Christmas hymns evoked a feeling he'd craved most of his life but which always escaped him. The feeling of love, of home, of family. Ever since he was a child, he'd wanted this—people to care about who cared about him. Faith. A reason to live a little better, bigger.

And he'd gotten it.

But how long would it last?

Courtney was leaving after Christmas, which was Friday. He was going to try to convince her to stay until after New Year's, but regardless, she'd be gone soon. In a few years, Wyatt would be off to college, and Treyvon would be graduating and getting a job somewhere.

Chase would be alone. In his big mansion on the lake. Would the view be as beautiful with no one to share it with?

The pastor was speaking about Mary's song when she visited Elizabeth. How her soul glorified the Lord for being mindful of her humble state.

Peace swept over him. All his fears drifted away. God had gotten him through the turmoil of having a baby out of wedlock, a tumultuous relationship with Missy, gaining custody of Wyatt, juggling a busy NFL career, forgiving Missy, dealing with her death, going after Len, and spending three years in prison. If God could forgive all that and still want Chase as His own, well, Chase had nothing to worry about.

He'd been blessed beyond belief. God could have given up on him a million times, but He hadn't.

And who was Chase to ask for more?

He'd been given more than enough.

The rest of the service passed quickly. When it ended, Treyvon and Wyatt headed up the aisle, but Courtney didn't stand.

Chase stayed seated next to her. Her face was drawn. She looked upset. "What's going on?"

"Do you mind if I sit here for a few minutes? You can go on without me. I won't be long."

She looked ready to shatter. He couldn't leave her alone like this. What had happened during the service to upset her?

He put his arm around her shoulders. "I'm not leaving you alone. I can tell you're upset. I'll stay right here with you."

She looked at him, and tears began dripping down her cheeks. Throwing her arms around his neck, she held him tightly, as small, silent sobs shook her body. He gently rubbed circles on her back, murmuring comfort. Her soft hair teased his cheek. He wanted to take away all her pain.

Finally, she sniffled and bent to pick up her purse. She found a tissue and dabbed at the tears.

"Sorry, I just…" Her eyes were bluer than he'd ever seen them. And sad. So sad.

"You don't have to say a thing. I'm here. Whatever you need."

"I've never spent Christmas without my mom. I can't imagine not having her sticky buns on Christmas morning. I miss buying presents for her. I'll never feel her arms around me or hear her voice again. It's hard. It's just so hard." She bowed her head, clearly emotional.

He drew her close. "I know, Courtney. It's unbelievably hard."

He had the most incredible urge to pray with her. He froze. Pray *with* her? Way out of his comfort zone.

But the feeling grew stronger until he couldn't ignore it.

Really, God?

"Would you mind if I prayed for you?" he asked.

She blinked in surprise. "I would like that."

"Heavenly Father, please comfort Courtney this Christmas season as she faces it without her mother. Let her hold tight to all the good memories and bless her with the comfort that someday she'll spend an eternity of Christmases with her mom. Amen."

"Amen."

He met her eyes, shining with gratitude, and he gulped.

And remind me You've already blessed me more than I could ever deserve. I won't be greedy and ask for more.

***

"What do you think of this, Courtney?" Wyatt held up a gold chain with a Christmas tree charm. After church, she, Chase, and Wyatt had driven to a shopping center to buy gifts. Treyvon had opted to stay home.

She shook her head. "Didn't you say Briana like silver?"

"Oh, yeah." He set the box back on the display. Then he wandered down the aisle where a stack of men's sweatshirts were piled. "Hey, I like this one."

Courtney snorted. *Boys.* One minute he was picking out a present for his maybe-girlfriend, the next he was shopping for himself. Chase had excused himself to find something in a different section, and she'd offered to help Wyatt. Being near Chase was incinerating her defenses. Clouding her reasoning. Making her think things she shouldn't. Like not moving to Indianapolis. Staying here...

"What about these?" Wyatt had crossed the aisle to the women's accessories. He held up a pair of socks.

"Can I ask you something?" She joined him, taking the socks out his hand and setting them back on the shelf.

"What?"

"How do you feel about this girl?"

His eyes got dreamy and a goofy grin spread across his face. It told her everything she needed to know.

"I like her," he said. "She's really pretty, but she's smart, too. Reads all the time. She's kind of quiet. But she's funny."

"Do you think giving her socks will tell her how you feel?" she asked gently.

He grimaced. "Uh..."

"Why don't you get her something that says you like her? A nice box of chocolates. An inexpensive piece of jewelry. Maybe something for the booklover inside—a witty mug or bookmark or something."

"You think?" He looked scared.

"You've been talking to her for how long?" Her fingers trailed a silky scarf as she waited for him to reply.

"About a month. I haven't asked her to be my girlfriend yet. We're just talking. But Owen has been talking to her, too."

She narrowed her eyes. "Is she playing you two against each other?"

"Briana?" He sounded shocked. "No way. I don't think she likes Owen at all."

"Then it's even more important for you to get her a gift that shows you care." She snapped her fingers. "Come on. Let's find the candy."

He fell in beside her as they dodged shoppers on the way to the candy section. After picking out a large box of assorted chocolates, a mug with Readers Gonna Read, and a simple silver bracelet with a book charm, they went to the wrapping paper aisle.

"You're good at this." Wyatt carried the gifts. "I'm glad you're here. Lauren always helps me with girl stuff, but she's been busy with the baby. I didn't want to bug her."

A warm glow filled her chest. "I'm sure she wouldn't think you're bugging her. But I'm happy to help. It's been fun for me."

"Do you have any presents to buy?" he asked.

As a matter of fact…she hadn't thought about it, but if she was spending Christmas with Chase…

"Yes. Maybe you can help me. What does Treyvon like?"

"Oh, easy. Music and food."

"So you're saying gift cards?"

He grinned. "That's exactly what he likes."

Courtney joked with Wyatt as they loaded up on gift cards, candy, and snacks. For a teen boy, he was remarkably easy to be with. She made a mental note to grab the sweatshirt he liked without him seeing it. But what could she get Chase?

She wanted to get him something to show her appreciation. No man had ever prayed for her out loud the way he had this morning. She wouldn't mind if he prayed for her more often. Like daily.

And those kinds of thoughts wouldn't do. Soon she'd have to stop the wishful thinking and concentrate on her future. She'd do what she'd always done—the right thing. Alone. In Indianapolis.

Chapter Eight

Chase spiraled a football in Drew's backyard Monday afternoon. Drew was a local firefighter, and today was his day off. Lauren, his wife, was inside with their baby, William. Courtney had stayed back at Chase's house to call a Realtor in Indianapolis. He didn't like it. But what could he say? *Don't leave. You don't need the job.* She wasn't his to keep.

"How is Courtney?" Drew asked.

"She's good. Sad, though. First Christmas without her mom."

"Must be tough on her." Drew tossed the ball back to him. "I always liked her. She was low key. No drama. Sweet."

"That's her." Sweet as the sugar cookies he'd helped her bake a few days ago. He sighed. It would be hard when she left.

"You look like you just lost the playoffs. What's up? Is she getting on your nerves? The stay a little too long?"

"No, not even close." He threw the ball to Drew. "It's complicated."

"Oh, I see." Drew smiled as if he had a secret.

"What?"

"You like her."

"No, I don't." He chucked the ball to Drew, who caught it easily. No surprise there since they'd been college roommates and both played on the football team.

"Yes, you do."

The ball crushed into Chase's chest. He wanted to spike it at Drew's head.

"Fine, I like her, but it's not like I can do anything about it."

"Why not?" Drew opened his hands. "Are you going to throw that back or not?"

He sailed it to Drew. "You know why."

"JJ?" He looked taken aback. "He's been gone for, what, three years?"

"It's more than JJ."

"I have no idea what you're talking about. Is it her? She's not into you? Doesn't want a relationship?"

Chase caught Drew's pass with a grunt. Did Courtney want a relationship? She didn't seem to mind being around him. Never flinched or scooted away from contact. They still talked for hours every day. But she was dead set on leaving, so he'd have to say a relationship wasn't on her radar.

"My priority is Wyatt." He didn't put enough power behind the ball, and it landed a few feet in front of Drew.

"Yeah, so?"

"And I went to prison."

"Um, I hate to break it to you, but she knows about the whole prison thing. Considering she wrote to you every week, I'd guess it isn't a deal breaker for her."

"It's a deal breaker for me."

Drew loped over to him. "It shouldn't be. You're free now. Keep it in the past."

"I'm not keeping it in the past." His voice rose. "I'm keeping it front and center so I don't make the same mistakes. When I think about how I hurt you, missed all those years with Wyatt, let my team down..." He hadn't gotten upset like this in a long time. He wanted to pump his fists in the air and shout.

Drew put his hand on his shoulder. "You've already apologized to me and Wyatt multiple times. You do put Wyatt first—have for years. I don't know why you're still punishing yourself. You're a good man. I mean, you took Treyvon in and you're paying for his college. It's over. Let it go."

Was it ever really over? Sometimes Chase woke up expecting to be on a narrow mattress, staring at the bars to his cell. The cycle of prison life had become so ingrained, it had taken him months not to automatically work out, read, and eat at exact times.

"Well, it doesn't matter. She's got a job. She'll be leaving soon."

Drew considered for a moment. "Are you going to the Sheffield's party?" Chase nodded. Drew continued. "Bring her with you. Show her Lake Endwell has the same kind of supportive network as the football community she used to love."

She *had* mentioned it being hard losing her football family. Chase straightened, nodding. "Tom invited her."

"See? There you go. Give her a reason to stay."

A reason to stay...maybe Drew was onto something. Chase wasn't enough to keep her there, but maybe a combination of things would do the trick. What did Courtney want?

A job. A home.

***

None of the houses she was researching excited her in the slightest. In fact, they all depressed her. Colonial in the suburbs. Condominium in the city. None of the homes were bad in themselves. But none of them were here.

She'd already booked a suite in an extended-stay hotel in Indianapolis. Maybe she'd wait to house hunt until she moved down there.

What she needed was a break. Stretching her back out, she scooped up Boo Boo, padded out of her room and went downstairs. The house was silent. Finally on Christmas break, Wyatt was hanging out at his best friend's house. Treyvon tended to stay in the guest cottage until dinner time. And Chase had gone to his friend Drew's. Courtney had always liked Drew. She was glad to hear he'd found happiness with his wife and baby son.

"Come on, Boo Boo. Let's sprawl out on the couch and watch romantic Christmas movies."

She'd learned early on in her marriage if JJ was home, football was on their television. After football season, basketball took center stage. Then hockey and baseball. It hadn't bothered her. She'd watch her programs when he was on the road or practicing. But old habits die hard. Here, at Chase's, it felt strange turning on the television to something *she* liked.

After fluffing a soft throw over her legs, she clicked the remote. Boo Boo circled her lap twice before curling up and falling asleep. She flipped through the channels until she found the one with the made-for-TV Christmas movies. A fake engagement to keep the female lead's job? Right up Courtney's alley. She snuggled into the couch.

About half an hour later, her eyes started to droop. The fake engagement story line was intriguing for sure, but months of scanty sleep had taken their toll. She couldn't help wondering what it would be like to have a fake engagement with Chase. Would he sneak a kiss the way the man in the movie did? And what would it feel like? It had been years and years since she'd kissed anyone but JJ. Frankly, it had been years since she'd kissed him, too.

She tried to stay awake...

Chase dominated her thoughts. His handsome face. Square jaw. Kind eyes. Fit body.

His integrity.

Funny how a convicted felon could have so much integrity...

She yawned, barely able to keep her eyes open.

He'd prayed for her...

Since the second she'd arrived, Chase had bent over backwards to help her out, to make her feel at home, to help her get through this tough time. What had she given him in return?

Had she given him anything?

Well, she'd helped brainstorm the juvenile program. And she'd made dinner. Baked cookies. Helped Wyatt shop. It wasn't much, but it was something.

She wanted to do more though.

She wanted...

To kiss him.

It had been so long since she'd been around a man, she must be losing it. She couldn't kiss Chase!

Couldn't date again. Couldn't marry again. Couldn't...

Suddenly wide awake, she shoved a throw pillow over her face and let out a muffled scream. It startled Boo Boo.

"Sorry, sweetie. Mama's having a crisis here. Go back to sleep." She petted him until the pooch let out a soft sigh.

Why couldn't she date again? Chase seemed interested. Didn't he?

And what happens if it doesn't work out?

She'd be right back to where she was now.

If she'd learned anything since JJ's death, it was that no one was going to figure life out for her. So what if the job she'd taken seemed as exciting as watching paint dry. She didn't *have* to work. She just needed something to occupy her time. Something she could get excited about.

Or would she ever be excited again?

God, I'm still here. And I don't know what to do. Taking care of Mom filled my time, but she's gone, too. Am I destined for a joyless existence? Or do You have something planned for me? Would You let me in on it, if You do?

Her eyes grew heavy again. The lady in the television movie had no idea how good she had it. A fake engagement was better than nothing. What Courtney wouldn't do for one more kiss...even a pretend one.

Chapter Nine

Chase opened the front door, and Boo Boo trotted to him. He picked up the little peanut. "Hey, did you miss me? Where's your mommy?"

Carrying the dog through the hall to the family room, he stopped short at the sight of Courtney asleep on the couch. A Christmas movie played on TV—one of those girly shows he never watched. A fuzzy gray throw covered her. Her blond hair had spread out across the throw pillow. Long lashes fanned on her cheeks.

He stood over the couch and stared at her. Couldn't help it. She was just that beautiful.

Boo Boo licked his cheek, snapping him out of his reverie. Great. He was officially becoming a creeper. Setting the dog on Courtney's lap, he sat beside her, reaching over to smooth the hair from her face. But the touch undid him, and he bent, kissing her cheek. A mere brush of his lips.

Her eyes opened, heavy with sleep, and her lips curved upward.

"Hey," she said.

"Hey." His throat felt lined with sandpaper.

"I must have dozed off." Propping on her elbows, she pushed up to a seated position, her legs still stretched along the couch. "How long has it been since you kissed someone?"

Had he heard her correctly? He straightened, itching to pace, but she tugged on his sleeve.

"Don't get up. Never mind. It was too personal. I'm sorry." She rubbed her right temple. He swallowed. Hard.

"Four and a half years." He clenched his jaw. Admitting it was…sobering.

"Really? It's been over three for me." She tucked her chin.

He tipped it up with his index finger. "It's hard on you, isn't it? Living without physical affection."

"Yeah." She toyed with the edge of the throw. "Don't know how much you miss it until it's gone."

"You're young. In your prime. You've got plenty of time for…" He couldn't finish the thought. Couldn't bear to think of her kissing another man.

She shook her head, her nose scrunching.

"What? You planning on staying single forever?" Would be a shame for someone with such a big heart to spend her life alone.

"I don't know."

"Don't you want kids?"

Those big blues widened, locking on him. Without a word, she nodded. Her face told him everything he needed to know. She wanted kids desperately. Muttering under his breath, he drew her into his arms.

"I'm sorry it didn't work out the way you wanted. You probably thought you and JJ would have a couple of little ones by now. You got a rotten deal."

She clung to him, the tension in her body slowly fading.

"You probably don't want more kids." She leaned back and gave him a tight smile. "You've got Wyatt."

"I've always wanted more. Always." It was true. He'd loved raising Wyatt. Would still love to have more kids. "But I never found the wife. After I became a Christian, I wouldn't even think about living the way I used to."

She bit her lower lip. "There were lots of women you could have dated. Married."

"I wanted love or nothing."

"I understand." Christmas music blared from a commercial on the television. "Chase?"

"What?"

"Would you kiss me?"

Warmth pooled in his gut. Kiss her? He'd like nothing more than to kiss her. Hadn't been able to stop thinking about it. But...

"Please?" Her voice sounded faraway.

He wouldn't make her beg.

Slowly, he wound his hand behind her neck, gazing into her eyes. He gave her every opportunity to change her mind. Heard her sharp intake of breath as he neared. Lowered his head, claimed her lips...

Sensations flooded him. Her mouth was plush, ripe. She tasted like sweetness. Freedom. Forever. Then she responded, and, as she pressed closer, his heartbeat pounded. He brought his other hand around her back, tugging her close. Her delicate body felt supple in his arms. All he could do was pour everything—all his gratitude, his affection, his emotions for her into the kiss.

This was what he'd been missing his entire life.

He'd experienced attraction, affection with Missy.

He'd never experienced love.

Until now.

He wanted to give Courtney his entire world. His time, his energy, his money, his life. All of it for her. If she'd just be his.

Madness. He had to stop. Had to put the brakes on before he did something stupid. Like tell her he loved her.

***

She sensed Chase retreating, but she wasn't ready. She kept her arms around his neck as he broke from their kiss.

What a kiss.

Slow, sensual—he hadn't rushed it. But the instant his lips had touched hers, she'd spiraled into the danger zone. Her pulse had sprinted out of control—was still zipping too fast—and all she'd been able to think was *don't let this end* and *I want to spend my life with him.*

His gray eyes looked as volatile as a thunderstorm. He was affected by their kiss, too. *Good.*

She traced his jaw, not taking her gaze from his. "I needed that. I think I've needed it since the second I arrived."

Maybe she shouldn't have admitted that. She didn't know where she stood, didn't want him thinking a kiss meant more than she could offer.

"If you need it again, just say the word." The corner of his mouth kicked into a wicked grin.

How did he know the perfect thing to say? She chuckled. "I might."

"I hope you do. Tonight. Tomorrow morning. In the afternoon…" He raised his eyebrows.

"You're incorrigible." She grabbed a throw pillow and swatted him with it. He laughed, taking it from her hands.

"And you're using too big of words for a jock like me." He watched her intently. "You're coming with me to the Sheffield party Wednesday, right?"

"Do you want me to come?"

"Yes. I do. Drew and Lauren will be there, too."

"What should I wear?" She hadn't brought anything formal.

"Something dressy, but not over the top. This is Lake Endwell, not a gala."

She mentally reviewed the clothes in her suitcase. She had a few options.

"Okay, then I'll come with you."

"Good." He stood. "I'm ordering pizza. We're staying in tonight."

She brought the throw up to her chin, smiling at Boo Boo. "Did you hear that? We're staying in." Nothing could make her happier.

A few minutes later, he returned, sitting next to her on the couch. "It will be here in thirty minutes."

She handed him the remote. "Here you go."

"What's wrong with this show?"

He was messing with her, wasn't he?

"Nothing," she said. "I figured you don't usually watch these types of movies." She waited for him to change the channel to ESPN or football. But he turned the volume up.

"Oh, good. There's a new one coming on." He grinned. "Looks like it has royalty."

She frowned as she studied him. Was he for real?

"What?" He looked innocent.

"Nothing," she said. "Nothing at all."

They watched the movie, critiquing the guy's acting skills and arguing over the girl's decision to sneak away for a while.

"I don't blame her." Courtney stuck her nose in the air. "His mother is treating her like she's a dumb bumpkin."

"But the prince needs her. He doesn't treat her like she's dirt." The doorbell rang. "Be right back."

As Chase paid for the pizza, the side door opened and Treyvon came into the family room. "Did you guys eat yet?"

Courtney jerked her thumb backward. "Chase is paying the pizza guy right now."

"Just in time." He grinned, dropping into a leather chair.

The scent of oregano and mozzarella hit them full force. Courtney drifted to the kitchen where Chase opened the boxes and set out paper plates and napkins.

"What were you up to today?" Chase asked Treyvon.

"Sleep. I'm reading a book, too. But hunger calls." He slid four slices onto his plate.

She and Chase helped themselves and brought their pizza back into the family room to resume the movie.

"What are you watching?" The look of horror on Treyvon's face was priceless.

"A Christmas movie." Chase acted as if watching it was the most natural thing in the world.

"Couldn't you find a game or something?"

"I'm sure one's on somewhere."

"So you're telling me you're *choosing* to watch this."

"Yeah." Chase bit into his pizza.

"Okay." Treyvon stood. "I'm out."

"Aw, come on. You can watch it with us."

"No way. I'd rather read." He waved to them and left.

Courtney burst into laughter. "Did you see his face when he realized what we were watching?"

Chase grinned. "Yeah. It's his loss. I think it's great."

His gaze told her he spoke the truth. Heady stuff—knowing he liked being with her.

"Me, too." She couldn't remember the last time she'd enjoyed an evening as much as this.

And it would be ending soon.

Christmas was a few days away. And then the real world called. But was Indianapolis her real world? It felt as foreign as Nigeria.

Christmas vacation would be over before she knew it. And then she would make a new home, a new life. She just wished she could muster up some enthusiasm about it.

Chapter Ten

"Are you almost ready?" Chase called up the staircase. He'd been dressed fifteen minutes ago. Courtney had yet to appear. He checked his watch. The drive to the restaurant wouldn't take long. It wasn't as if they were late. He was just antsy. At least Courtney had agreed to come with him to the party. It was adults only, so Wyatt and Treyvon were hanging out at home, wrapping Christmas presents. Wyatt and Treyvon shuffled in next to them. Poinsettias lined the front of the sanctuary, and two tall Christmas trees twinkled up there, too. Piano music played as people quietly found seats. All morning he'd been wired and tense. Spending all this time with Courtney had been like nothing he'd ever experienced. He'd never gotten so close to a woman, never shared his emotions and hopes. Not even with Missy. But Courtney had loosened something inside him.

Maybe they should skip the party.

Movement above caught his eye. Courtney, in an ice blue sweater and cream slacks, descended the staircase. Her hair lay in big curls down her back, and her makeup accented her pretty features. When she made it to the bottom, he noted she was a few inches taller than usual. High heels. He almost groaned.

"You look stunning."

She smiled, dimples flashing. "Thank you. You clean up pretty good yourself."

He gestured to his thin dark gray sweater and matching gray dress pants. "This old thing?"

She laughed. "I thought that was supposed to be my line."

"No one would believe it. You're beautiful."

"Thank you." A faint blush rose to her cheeks. He helped her into her coat then led her out to the garage and into his truck. As he started it, he suddenly felt tongue-tied, out of his element. He fumbled around for something to talk about.

"I did some research on current programs for kids coming out of juvenile detention as adults." Chase placed his hand behind her seat and looked back as he reversed out of the drive. "I didn't see any for this part of Michigan."

"You might want to call the director, or whoever is in charge of the detention center, and ask what current support systems they have for kids."

"I was thinking the same."

They continued to volley ideas as they drove around the lake. The streetlights and glow of windows cheered up the winter night. Soon he parked outside the restaurant, then opened the passenger door for her.

"I'd better warn you not everyone is ecstatic I moved here." He tucked her arm under his as they crossed the paved lot.

"Well, I'm glad you moved here." Her smile almost made him stumble.

"I appreciate it but, be prepared for comments. If you feel uncomfortable at any time, say the word and we'll leave."

She patted his arm. "I was married to an NFL player, remember? I can handle it."

He followed her inside. Twinkle lights were everywhere. Upbeat Christmas music played, and clusters of people milled about, laughing and talking. Chase hung their coats on a rack then led Courtney to where he spotted Drew and Lauren.

"Hey, you made it!" Drew half-embraced him then turned to Courtney. "It is good to see you." He hugged her. "Courtney, this is my wife, Lauren. Lauren, this is Courtney Trudesta. She was married to JJ Trudesta, one of Chase's former teammates."

"Welcome to Lake Endwell." Lauren's big smile reached her eyes. "I'm so glad you came out tonight."

Chase kissed Lauren's cheek. "Who's watching William?"

"Mom's babysitting." Lauren grinned. "She's taken to the role of grandma like a champ." She turned to Courtney. "The baby doesn't sleep much, so if I yawn, forgive me."

Courtney laughed. "I understand."

"Let me introduce you around." Chase took Courtney by the hand. "We'll be back in a few minutes."

He spotted the Sheffield brothers in the center of the room. He kept Courtney close to him as he made the introductions.

"Good to see you made it." Tom clapped him on the back. "It's great to meet you, Courtney."

Bryan nodded to them and introduced himself. Sam joked to Courtney about coming in the wrong season since the lake was best in the summer.

"You have to meet my wife, Stephanie," Tom said, trying to wave down a gorgeous brunette.

"Jade, too." Bryan scanned the room. "If you spot a tiny redhead, you've found my wife."

"And Celeste." Sam pointed to a cluster of women. "There. With Aunt Sally. They're all plotting something. I can feel it. Claire and Libby, too."

Tom snagged the sleeve of the man who joined them. "This is our brother-in-law, Reed. He's married to our sister, Claire."

Chase was impressed how easily Courtney handled all the introductions. Soon, a group of women—all Sheffields—joined them, engaging Courtney in conversation. Chase's chest swelled in thankfulness. He'd gotten to know them bit by bit, and they'd been kind to him. To have them welcome Courtney like this? More than he ever expected.

Thank You, Lord. These people have shown me nothing but kindness when I deserved none.

He frowned as a thought occurred. If all of them accepted him, knowing what he'd done, why was he so convinced he was all wrong for Courtney?

***

"I think I gained five pounds tonight." Courtney pushed her empty dessert plate away and took another drink of her coffee.

"Five? I'm pushing at least ten." Lauren polished off a slice of tiramisu. "I'm going in for another round. Hopefully, the cheerleaders will still recognize me next fall."

"Cheerleaders?"

Lauren chuckled. "I'm the high school coach."

"Oh, that sounds fun."

"I love it. We have a great group of girls. You'll have to come to a game this year. Can I get you anything while I'm up?"

Courtney shook her head. Lauren was the kind of woman Courtney would love to get to know better. Genuine. Chase and Drew had excused themselves a few minutes earlier to say hello to someone Drew worked with. With Lauren on her way to the dessert table, Courtney took the opportunity to people watch. Everyone had been friendly and nice to her. The Sheffield ladies had pressed her to come back and visit soon. And the aunt—Aunt Sally—had hugged Courtney for so long, she'd thought maybe they'd met before or something. The short woman was clearly a spitfire. She wore dangling Christmas bulb earrings that lit up. Sally had told Courtney if she needed anything—anything at all—to just holler. Courtney had the feeling she truly meant it.

Someone bumped her chair. "Oops, sorry." A thin brunette wearing a skin-tight cheetah print dress narrowed her eyes. "I don't recognize you."

The tone bordered on rude, but Courtney pasted a smile on. She'd dealt with many beautiful women who'd had designs on JJ. "I'm Courtney Trudesta."

"I thought I saw you with Chase." The woman's heavily lined eyes widened and she waved her finger. "You'd better be careful. He's trouble."

"Oh, you know him?" Courtney kept her tone pleasant. She wasn't buying this woman's advice.

"Everyone knows about him." She leaned in. "He just got out of prison."

"You don't say? I'll take it into consideration."

She made a sour face. "Don't you want details?"

Courtney blinked sweetly. "I don't need them."

"Your loss." She sauntered away.

"What was that all about?" Chase stood next to the table. She hadn't noticed him come up.

Her heartbeat skipped at the intensity in his eyes. "No clue."

"I can guess." Regret washed over his face.

She covered his hand. "Hey, people have always talked about you. When you were playing football, some fans loved you, and others said terrible things. They did the same to JJ."

"But that didn't bother me. I couldn't change what they thought about my performance."

"And you still can't."

His gray eyes captured hers. "I want to. I want to be...I don't know." He swiped his eyebrow with his finger.

"What were you going to say?" She hoped he would finish the thought and stop living with so much regret.

"It doesn't matter."

"It does to me."

His jaw clenched. She couldn't remember seeing him this vulnerable before.

"I want to go back and do things different."

"You can't. The only thing you can do is move forward."

Much like herself. She'd be moving forward to another city, but after meeting all these kind, fun people, she wished she could stay. Lauren was easy to be with. The Sheffield women reminded her of the football wives she used to hang out with—except the Sheffields seemed less competitive.

She'd lost her support group after JJ died. Eventually, they'd all gone on with their lives, and she couldn't blame them. Nothing lasted forever.

If she could go back would she do things different?

Was she willing to take the advice she'd given Chase? Was moving to Indianapolis really moving forward?

Yes. Staying here is out of the question. I've had the love of a lifetime. It doesn't happen twice.

She lunged for her coffee. Too much to reflect on. Tonight was to enjoy.

Chapter Eleven

A few hours later, Chase led Courtney by the hand to the family room's couch. All night his nerves had been twitchy. As the evening had worn on, he'd had one thought.

Ask her to stay.

He plugged in the Christmas tree lights then flipped the switch to the gas fireplace. As the flames burst upward and the tree twinkled, he selected a playlist of slow songs. "Can I get you anything?"

"No." She sat on the couch, one leg crossed over the other.

He returned to the couch, sitting next to her.

"So...what did you think of everyone?"

Her lips were close. He couldn't stop staring at them.

"Really nice. Fun. I liked them a lot."

"And Lake Endwell?" His voice sounded husky. He didn't care. Her perfume was killing him.

"Charming," she practically purred. "Delightful."

He took her hand in his. "What if you didn't move to Indianapolis?" As soon as he uttered the question, his gut clenched. What if she hated the idea?

"What would I do instead?" Her eyelashes fluttered.

"Join me in starting the program. You know what you're doing. I don't. Name your position on the board. I'll pay you."

She scooted away slightly. "The program. Right."

Had he said something wrong? "You need something to fill your time. I do, too. We've already made so much progress together."

She stood, turning her back to him. He rose, too.

"I can find lots of things to fill my time, Chase."

He placed his hands on her shoulders. She flinched. Had she changed her mind about him at the party? What was he doing wrong?

His insides screamed to tell her the truth, to tell her he loved her. But the words were choking him.

"This is coming out wrong." He wiped his hand down his cheek. "I want you to stay. Not because I think you need a job or to use you for my program or anything."

She faced him then, her eyes wide, questioning. "Why?"

Tell her!

"I...I..." He balled his hands down at his sides. "Well, the truth is, Courtney, I care about you very much."

Questions swam in her eyes. "Is this the kind of care a friend would feel for his friend's widow?"

When she said it like that, he felt like a jerk. He shouldn't have these feelings for his friend's widow.

"No," he said. "Not exactly."

"Then what?"

"Like this." He cupped her face and slowly leaned forward. His lips grazed hers. He looked into her eyes. "Tell me when to stop."

She didn't say a word.

He kissed her again, holding her close, trying to convey his feelings as best as he could. Was he getting through to her? Did she have any clue how much she meant to him?

He ended the kiss, not moving away from her for fear she'd leave.

"I didn't mean to, but somewhere along the line, reading all your letters, spending time with you here…" He wanted to say it, needed to say it, but the words wouldn't come out. Come on, man, say it. "I fell in love with you. Courtney, I love you."

He'd never said those words to a woman. Not once. Because he'd never meant them until now.

"I…" She turned to face the tree, crossing her arms over each other. "I don't know what to say."

"Please stay."

***

Courtney's heartbeat was thumping faster than a drum solo at a rock concert. Did Chase really love her?

Could she stay?

She closed her eyes briefly, imagining life in Lake Endwell with him. Starting the program together. Laughing and enjoying Treyvon and Wyatt. Becoming friends with Lauren. Getting to know the Sheffield women. And she wanted it so bad it almost crushed her.

"I can't," she whispered.

"Why not?" His voice was low, controlled.

"Because it's too good to be true, Chase." She spun to him. "Don't you see this is all sugarplums and Christmas wishes?"

"It doesn't have to be. Maybe it's a second chance. For both of us. We can make this last. We can—"

"No, we can't." She saw it all clearly now. She'd come here vulnerable. Desperate. She'd fallen in love with him through his letters, too. But it was wrong. All of this was wrong.

She'd had her love of a lifetime, and he'd died, leaving her alone.

She was meant to be alone.

The muscle in his cheek flickered. "Why did you stop writing?"

"Because I needed to stop. I relied on it too much. I…I was falling for you."

"I see." He sounded crushed.

"No, you don't." She shook her head, her hair swinging. "I know you well enough to guess what you're thinking. You think I deserve better, that I could never go for someone who went to prison, someone who tried to murder a man. But you're wrong. That's not why I have to leave."

His eyes darkened. "Then why are you?"

She covered her eyes, hating the fact she hadn't realized this earlier. "Because lightning doesn't strike twice. I had my happily ever after."

"It didn't last ever after, though." He frowned.

"But I had it once. I'm sorry. I can't do this. I just can't."

She ran upstairs, could hear his footsteps thumping behind her. When she got to her room, she tried to shut the door, but she wasn't fast enough. His hand pushed it open.

"Why?" He followed her inside.

"I buried JJ. And my mom."

"Is that what you're worried about? You won't bury me."

She scoffed, waving indifferently. "Typical. Mr. Football. Indestructible."

"I never said that."

"It's how you are, though. You're strong. You tempt me so much. Too much."

"What's so terrible about that?" He caressed her upper arms. "I love you. Didn't you hear me?"

She backed up. He stepped forward. She kept inching back until she touched the wall. He leaned in.

"I...I need to leave." She licked her lips. "I can't start over here."

"Why? Because you might actually be happy?"

She nodded, her defenses leveled. Tears threatened, but she squeezed them away.

He muttered something, slid his arm around her waist and gently pulled her to him. "I don't know what to do with you, Courtney."

"Just let me go. Forget about me."

"I could never forget you. Will never forget you. Don't ask me to. It's impossible."

"Chase, please?" Tears fell from her eyes. Why was he so perfect? If he'd just sulk or get mad or something, this would be so much easier.

"Don't cry." He wiped the tears away with his thumb. "I'll leave you alone. But please, Courtney, don't leave tonight. Sleep on it."

"I'm not changing my mind." She thrust her chin out, hating that it trembled.

"I can't change my heart." He gave her a sad look then turned and walked out, shutting the door behind him.

Boo Boo let out a yip at her feet. She picked him up, cradling him to her chest, and let the tears fall.

Chase McGill loved her.

And she hadn't even told him she loved him, too.

She'd dismissed him instead.

It was for the best.

Doing the right thing had never felt so wrong.

CHAPTER TWELVE

He shouldn't have told her his feelings, shouldn't have pressured her to stay. Chase raked his fingers through his hair. Shoulders hunched, he sat on the edge of his bed. The clock ticked to one thirty-five a.m. Why had he ever thought someone like Courtney, who had a heart of solid gold, would want to pursue a relationship with him?

Oh sure, she said she'd had happily ever after once and that she'd been falling for him through his letters, but he wasn't stupid. He could read between the lines. She'd had a stand-up guy in JJ. And she'd only grown feelings for Chase because she'd been lonely.

Letters weren't flesh and blood, anyhow. If they were, they'd have told her his deepest secret. He'd never told anyone what happened the day he tracked down Len. The instant he'd driven his truck into the guy, he'd regretted it. Felt sick to his stomach at the burning rage which had led him there. He could have backed up and ran Len over again, finished the job, but he'd put the truck in park, lowered his forehead to the steering wheel and sobbed at what he'd become.

A monster.

And, yeah, he'd spent four years repenting, improving himself through prayer and reading and helping others, but underneath it all, a monster still lurked.

Because if anyone ever threatened Courtney...he'd have to wrestle with his rage all over again, and he didn't know if he could tame the monster inside him.

It never really left. It was part of him.

He dropped his chin, folded his hands.

God, I love her, and I want her to stay more than anything. I want to protect her and spend my days with her. I would love nothing more than to have a house full of babies with that woman. But I know who I am. And maybe she's right to leave. She's better off without me.

A Bible verse he'd memorized in prison came to mind. Ephesians 2: 8. "For it is by grace you have been saved, through faith, and this is not from yourselves, it is the gift of God—not by works, so that no one can boast."

Okay, I know I can't earn Your love. I get it. You know the monster in me, and You love me anyway. But I also know sin has consequences. My sins have been many. This is one of the consequences.

Who was he to ask her to stay? To tell her he loved her? To expect her to drop her plans and move to Lake Endwell?

Arrogance had always been his downfall. The take-charge, high-adrenaline, give-it-everything side of him had gotten him far in football, but this wasn't a sport.

He scooted back and sprawled on his bed, staring up at the ceiling. Courtney's words from last week echoed in his head. *"You paid the price. You can move on with your life."*

Had he paid the price? Or was he paying it now?

Her tears, her plea for him to forget about her was shredding his heart.

How was he supposed to move on without her?

The row of books on his dresser caught his eye. He'd read each one of them multiple times in prison. Strange, but sometimes when he'd been reading in his cell, he'd felt an absolute peace. He'd been able to drown out the distractions. Prayer had come easily, too. He'd become convinced he could do all things through Christ, who strengthened him. And one of those things was to put his loved ones first, especially Wyatt. To consider his son's needs before his own.

Wasn't that what love was all about?

How did Wyatt feel about Courtney?

He shot up to a seated position. Wyatt liked her. Chase knew it. They got along great. Wyatt wouldn't be a problem.

But what were Courtney's needs?

Love wasn't mere words. Love was action.

By asking her to stay, he'd unintentionally hurt her. He hadn't realized burying her loved ones had made her wary of falling in love again, but it clearly had. And she was taking a big step by moving to Indianapolis. Maybe it was wrong of him to expect her to stay, to change her plans.

As usual, he'd been thinking of his own needs, his desires.

Okay, God, I'm a slow learner, but I think I get it. Courtney can't help having fears about losing her loved ones. Help me accept it. She was a bright light for me during my darkest time. I want to be that for her, unworthy as I am. Please guide me. Whatever happens tomorrow, I know You'll work it out for my good.

He just wished Courtney wouldn't leave. If only things had worked out differently for both of them. If he could grant her one wish, he knew she'd ask for JJ back, and even if Chase could give her that, he wouldn't. Couldn't pretend to even want to.

He'd never be JJ Trudesta.

He was Chase McGill. Father, friend, former football star, and convicted felon. And he couldn't change it.

***

She'd been wrong to come here.

Courtney carefully folded another sweater and stacked it in her suitcase. She hadn't attempted to sleep. It was well past midnight.

She'd hurt the one man who understood her better than her own husband had. Not that it was JJ's fault. She'd opened up to Chase in her letters, been vulnerable in a way she'd never been before, not even with JJ. And Chase had never minded her honesty. In fact, each letter he'd written back had held some insight, some positive way to look at life. She'd read them over and over, carefully keeping them in a pretty box. She hadn't been able to stand the thought of them stuck in a storage shed, so she'd brought them with her. They were in her trunk.

She loved Chase McGill.

She'd fallen in love with him long before she'd ever parked in his driveway. She just hadn't wanted to admit it to herself.

Her heart was shriveling. She could actually feel it caving in. And she deserved the pain.

She needed to leave. Had she left anything in the bathroom? She scanned the counter. No. All her makeup and toiletries were in her bag. There would be no trace of her come tomorrow.

She sighed. She couldn't up and leave right now. She owed it to Chase to wait until morning the way he'd asked.

But what if he broke down her last defenses? What if he convinced her to stay?

Lord, I know it's cowardly of me to want to sneak out, but You know what I'm up against. He's everything I want. A Christian man who is kind and thoughtful. Gorgeous. Strong. I don't even know who I am anymore. How can I possibly think about a relationship with him? What if he realizes I'm not as great as my letters made me seem? What if I moved here—which I'm not going to do—and he got tired of me? We broke up? I couldn't bear to live in this ideal place and make friends here if it won't last. I'm so scared.

A raging headache was in her future. She could feel it coming.

She wished her mother was here to talk her through this. *Mom, what would you say?*

It would start with *"You're God's child, Courtney, so don't ever doubt your identity. You'll never get it from money, a relationship, a job, or anything other than Him. What are you so scared about? The man loves you. You love him. End of story."*

But it wasn't that easy. Because Courtney's stories ended with funerals.

She zipped her suitcase shut.

Lord, Mom always told me I am Your child. And I know it. I can only find myself in You.

She was beloved by the One who made the sun, moon, and stars.

Sitting on the edge of the bed, she pinched the bridge of her nose. If she was beloved by God, why was she running from the man who loved her?

Lord, You already gave me love once. And it was great. I loved JJ with all my heart. I don't know why I'm even thinking about Chase.

The emotions she'd dammed earlier sprung a leak. Visions of the day she married JJ flew through her memory. The feeling of complete love, absolute bliss as she'd said, "I do." The fight about where to place the couch when they'd moved into their first house. The lonely nights when he was on the road. The sense of rightness when he'd return and hold her in his arms.

God, I did love him. And I want You to tell him so. Tell him I loved him with all my heart and soul. But my heart is still beating here, and I don't want him to think I didn't love him. I did. He's just...gone. And I can't have him back. And, Lord, don't tell him this—this is only between You and me. I don't want him back. I'm in love with Chase. Forgive me for my disloyalty. Oh, God, please forgive me.

She curled onto her side, sobbing. She let it all out. Her anger toward herself for falling in love with another man. Her anger at JJ for dying. Her loneliness without her mom. And when she'd cried every tear she had, she wiped her eyes and hugged herself.

She knew what she had to do. And she would. Tomorrow.

CHAPTER THIRTEEN

Chase bolted awake. What time was it? He glanced at the clock, relieved it showed five forty-seven a.m. Courtney hadn't left yet, had she? He shot out of bed, peeked out the window and sighed in relief that her car was parked in the drive. It meant he still had a chance. And he wasn't going to botch it this time.

After a quick shower, he toweled off his hair and threw on a pair of jeans and a long sleeved T-shirt. Then he tiptoed downstairs and brewed a pot of coffee. He had some thinking to do before she woke up.

Courtney had been dealt a series of heavy blows, and he wasn't about to let her leave here as tired and lonely as she'd arrived. Although it was risky, he was determined to be the friend she needed, even if it meant a lifetime of only being pen pals.

Did he want more?

Yes.

But he'd accept her decision.

He just prayed he could get through to her someday and win her love. It might take years, but he had the rest of his life to try.

He poured a mug of coffee, slipped his feet into shoes and went out onto the deck. A fresh coat of snow covered everything. He stared out at the evergreens dusted with sparkling snow. Everything around him shimmered in white. Stunning.

Lord, help me find the right words to say to Courtney. Don't let my selfish impulses take over. Let me be like You.

The swoosh of the patio door startled him. He looked over his shoulder. Courtney slowly walked toward him.

A wave of love almost knocked him over. Her hair was loose, her face free from makeup. She wore a white sweater, dark jeans, and boots. Her face looked pinched, worried. He braced himself for whatever she was about to say.

"Merry Christmas Eve," she said.

Hadn't expected that. He nodded, trying not to appear too earnest or intense. "Merry Christmas Eve."

Neither spoke for a few moments. How should he broach the subject? He knew what he needed to tell her, but he didn't have the words. Finally, he took a deep breath, set his mug on the rail, and turned to face her.

"I'm sorry, Courtney. I shouldn't have dumped all my feelings on you last night, and I certainly shouldn't have pressured you to change your plans. I know this move to Indianapolis wasn't easy for you to make. You deserve a fresh start down there. I was selfish."

She blinked, clearly surprised.

"You didn't dump your feelings on me, Chase. We've both been fighting it since I arrived. I don't think either of us can deny our chemistry."

He shifted his jaw. "I hope you don't think it's merely a physical thing for me. It's more. Much more. It's your soul—who you are—that I'm attracted to. In love with. I know you don't want to hear it, and I don't blame you. But, I have something more to say."

She hugged herself.

"Before I go on, though, I need to tell you the truth about the day I went after Len."

Her eyes widened.

"I'd hired a private investigator when he'd skipped bail. The police couldn't find him. My investigator did." He clenched his jaw. "I drove up to the Upper Peninsula, saw him standing in the driveway, and I lost it. I drove my truck right into him."

"Oh, Chase."

"The impact threw him to the ground. When I saw him holding his leg in agony, I realized what I'd become. A monster, Courtney. An absolute monster."

Reaching up, she trailed her finger down his cheek. "Oh, Chase."

He backed up. "If someone hurt you...I don't know. I guess what I'm trying to say is the monster is still there."

"But you didn't kill Len." Her head tipped to the side ever so slightly, and her expression was a gentle as a lamb.

"I could have. I wanted to. I tried."

"So why didn't you get out and beat him up? Shoot him? Run him over again?"

He inhaled a shaky breath. "As soon as I hit him, I regretted it. I broke down. I've never felt so ashamed in my life."

"I'm so sorry, Chase." She put both hands around his neck and held him tightly.

"You aren't disgusted?"

Still holding him, she stared up into his eyes. "I'm not. You aren't a monster." Then she shivered.

"You're cold." He gestured to the door. "Let's take this inside."

They headed back into the kitchen. She sat at the island as Chase poured her a cup of coffee, sliding the cream and sugar tray to her.

"Look, Courtney, I've never been in love before, so bear with me. I know you loved JJ with all your heart. I admire that about you. And I know you're not over him. I don't blame you. He was special. But he's not here. And I'm not JJ. I never will be. I get it. You're moving to Indianapolis, and I'm going to miss you. I really want you to stay. To explore a relationship with me. We're a good team. Together we could change lives, but I don't expect you to agree. I'm going to ask you for one thing, though."

Her hands clutched the mug. She hadn't reacted. He couldn't read her.

He didn't like it.

"What?" she asked. "What's the one thing?"

"Let me keep writing to you. And, I know this is a lot to ask, but please keep writing to me." He wanted to take her in his arms, but he kept his feet cemented to the floor. "I know you need to make a life, and I do, too. Your letters, your words helped me get this far. Please don't take them away from me, Courtney."

***

As if her heart could take another battering... Courtney bowed her head as his words sank in.

He humbled her.

She lifted her gaze, trying to convey everything he needed to understand. "You're right. You're not JJ."

A shadow passed over his face.

"But you're wrong to think I'm not over him." She took a moment to get the words right. "I loved him very much."

"I know."

"And I love you very much. I can honestly say that."

His jaw dropped.

"Yes, I love you, Chase McGill. I felt guilty for having all these feelings for you, but I didn't realize it until last night. I thought I was being disloyal to JJ. I'll probably feel that way for a while."

"I can understand that."

She tilted her head. "I know. You're the one person who could understand it. It's why I kept writing. I didn't want to think I was falling in love. I just knew your letters were precious to me. And then you invited me here, and I almost felt like I was cheating on JJ."

He let out a soft laugh, rubbing the back of his neck. "I didn't realize."

"Neither did I. But last night I prayed about it. And I made peace with it. I want you to know you will never be second place in my heart. You've had first place for a long time."

"Does this mean...?" He gazed at her with so much love, her knees wobbled.

"I'll stay?" She nodded. "Yes, I think Lake Endwell is the perfect fit. I'll rent a condo. But I'll probably be here a lot. Can you handle that?"

"Can I?" He was at her side at lightning speed. He lifted her off the stool and kissed her. This was where she belonged.

She kissed him back, reveling in all the strength keeping her upright. How long they held each other, she had no idea. Finally, they broke free, staring into each other's eyes.

"We won't rush it." Chase brushed her hair from her face. "We'll date. Do the boyfriend/girlfriend thing. Take it as slow as you need."

"And the job you offered me?" She locked her hands around his neck.

"I can't start the program without you." He kissed her again.

"You could, but it will be more fun together."

"Everything is more fun with you. I love you, Courtney."

"I love you, too, Chase."

"Then what do you say we make some of your mom's famous sticky buns before Wyatt and Treyvon wake up?"

Her heart was ready to burst. Leave it to Chase to remember the sticky buns. "I would love that."

"On second thought, why don't we practice the boyfriend/girlfriend thing for a while longer?" He pulled her into his arms again.

"Okay, but only for a little while. The dough will need time to rise."

"Merry Christmas, sweetheart."

Epilogue

One year later...

Chase did one last check. His dress pants were pressed. Shirt and tie just right. Cologne not too overpowering. Classical jazz played on the speakers.

"She didn't suspect a thing." Wyatt peeked out the front window. "I told her we bought a present for Boo Boo and she might as well leave him here until after church. Wait, I think it's her. Kill the lights!"

The house went dark.

"Not the Christmas tree lights, Treyvon."

Chase pressed his hand to his forehead. This wasn't going as planned.

"Sorry," Treyvon yelled. Wyatt ran to the family room. "Come on, Treyvon, let's get out of here. Break a leg, Dad."

Everything was in place. The past year had been the best of his life. He and Courtney had done all the paperwork and legal filings to start Trudesta Way, a six month after-release program for eighteen-year-olds leaving juvenile detention centers. Together, they'd talked to a variety of directors, juvenile delinquents, and potential mentors. With Courtney's tenacity, they'd scored enough donations to fund the program for a full year. And Chase couldn't wait to mentor his first person.

The front door opened. "Hello? Where are you? Chase? Why is it so dark in here?"

"Back here, Court." He wiped his sweaty palms down his pants. It was go time.

"What are you doing in the dark?" Courtney shook her head, but she was smiling. She came up to where he stood in the middle of the family room, reached up on her tiptoes and gave him a kiss.

"Waiting for you." He put his hands on either side of her waist.

"We need to get going if we're going to make the Christmas Eve service."

"We've got time." He searched her eyes, sparkling with love and Christmas joy. "I have an early Christmas present."

"You do?"

"Uh-huh." He gave her a grin. "Boo Boo, come here boy."

The tiny dog galloped to him. Chase picked him up. "Good dog. Now do you have something for your mommy?"

Boo Boo licked his face. Chase laughed, handing the dog to Courtney. With suspicion streaming from her gaze, she held the itty-bitty mutt.

Chase dropped to one knee. "Courtney, my love, the breath of fresh air I will always need, my favorite pen pal, you know I love you."

She was blinking rapidly. "I know."

"One year ago, I told you we'd do the boyfriend/girlfriend thing. Take it slow. It's been the best year of my life."

"Mine too," she whispered.

"But, this year has taught me one thing." He stared up at her. "I need more than a girlfriend. I'm ready for a wife. Courtney Trudesta, will you marry me?"

She gasped, almost dropping Boo Boo. "Yes! Oh, yes, Chase! I'll marry you."

"Check Boo Boo's collar."

"Why?" She fumbled with his collar. "It's not tick season."

Then she saw the sparkling diamond ring dangling from the collar. She took it off, and Chase slid it on her finger.

"I love you, Courtney."

"I love you, Chase." She hugged him. "Merry Christmas."

"To a lifetime of merry Christmases and a house full of babies."

She raised her eyebrows. "I like the way you think."

"Plenty more where that came from." He took her in his arms and kissed her. The Christmas lights twinkled around them. Snow fell outside. And Boo Boo danced at their feet.

His Christmas wish had come true. Thank the good Lord for second chances.

The End

ACKNOWLEDGMENTS

Many thanks to Belle Calhoune, who approached me with a delightful opportunity to contribute to the Christmas novella collection, *I'll Be Home for Christmas.* Thank you to Belle, Allie Pleiter, and Lenora Worth for all their hard work in promoting the collection to a best-seller spot several weeks in a row.

Thank you to my proofreader, Judy, who catches my goofy mistakes and is always a true professional.

Thank you to my readers! I appreciate each and every one of you for taking time to read my stories.

Finally, thank you to my Lord and Savior, Jesus Christ. You're the reason we celebrate Christmas. May we never forget it.

Dear Reader

Dear Reader,

After writing about Drew and Lauren falling in love in ***Hometown Hero's Redemption***, I had several readers ask for Chase's story. Wyatt was just a ten-year-old kid trying to adjust to life in Lake Endwell with his guardian, Drew, after Chase went to prison. I had so much fun returning to these characters as well as checking in with the Sheffield siblings. While Chase made a lot of mistakes in his past, his faith made him want to live a better life. It's easy to feel undeserving of love, but that's the beauty of being God's child. Jesus paid the price for our sins. Love is a free gift. I hope you're filled with Christmas joy this holiday season. God bless you!

Jill Kemerer

About the Author

Jill Kemerer is a Publisher's Weekly bestselling, multi-published author of Christian romance novels and Christian nonfiction. Her essentials include coffee, M&Ms, a stack of books, her miniature-dachshund, and taking long nature walks. She resides in Ohio with her husband and two almost-grown children. Jill loves connecting with readers, so please visit her website, jillkemerer.com.

MORE BOOKS BY JILL KEMERER

Wyoming Cowboys Series
Book 1: *The Rancher's Mistletoe Bride*
Book 2: *Reunited with the Bull Rider*
Book 3: *Wyoming Christmas Quadruplets*
Book 4: *His Wyoming Baby Blessing*

Lake Endwell Series
Book 1: *Small-Town Bachelor*
Book 2: *Unexpected Family*
Book 3: *Her Small-Town Romance*
Book 4: *Yuletide Redemption*
Book 5: *Hometown Hero's Redemption*

Nonfiction
Game On: The Christian Parents' Sport Survival Guide

Made in the USA
Las Vegas, NV
11 April 2021